Chocolate S.O.S

SUE LIMB

BLOOMSBURY

LONDON BERLIN NEW YORK SYDNEY

Bloomsbury Publishing, London, Berlin, New York and Sydney

First published in Great Britain in January 2012 by Bloomsbury Publishing Plc
50 Bedford Square, London, WC1B 3DP

A CIP catalogue record for this book is available from the British Library

ISBN 978 0 7475 9917 3

MIX
Paper from
responsible sources
FSC® C018072

Typeset by Hewer Text UK Ltd, Edinburgh
Printed in Great Britain by Clays Ltd, St Ives plc, Bungay, Suffolk

1 3 5 7 9 10 8 6 4 2

www.bloomsbury.com
www.JessJordan.co.uk

Chocolate S·O·S

For Anna Wednesday Meyers

Chapter 1

'No!' breathed Flora. 'I can't believe it! You and Fred haven't really split up, have you, babe? *Really?*'

'Really!' Jess said sternly. 'Really, really, really, really, *really*!'

'But he was so funny in the hosting routine you did last night!'

Jess was silent for a moment – silent with a kind of white-hot, boiling, deep, volcanic rage. She hadn't told Flora yet what a terrible thing Fred had done.

'Oh yes!' The words burst out of Jess's mouth in a stream of fury. 'He was absolutely hilarious, wasn't he? Absolutely side-splitting. Ha, ha, ha!'

Flora stared in amazement at Jess's harsh tone. 'What . . . ?' she faltered.

'He'd left me to organise the whole dinner dance on my own, a week before the event! He said he was "resigning from the committee". Hah! What committee? We were supposed to be running it together, just him and me. So basically what he meant was that he was dumping me in it and refusing to help me any more with *anything*. That was bad enough!'

Flora winced in sympathy.

'So I told him I'd do the whole thing myself,' Jess ranted on. 'And that included the stand-up routine for the hosting bits, obviously. I mean, you can't plan and rehearse a hosting routine if you're not speaking to each other, can you? Besides, Fred had flu all last week. He wasn't at school, so I just naturally assumed the hosting bit was totally my responsibility.'

'Awesome!' murmured Flora, gazing at Jess in admiration.

'Yes. Well, I worked on my Cinderella routine, right?'

'Right!' Flora nodded. 'And it was brilliant!'

'I showed you bits while I was writing it, didn't I? I really enjoyed working on that – you know, some great jokes just kind of bubbled up in my mind and I was *so* looking forward to performing it. Then, on the night, what happens? I nerved myself, stepped out into the spotlight and when I was only a couple of lines into my routine, Fred appeared from nowhere, dressed like a freakin' amoeba, and jumped up on stage!'

'You mean . . .' Flora was struggling to get her head around this. 'You mean that wasn't rehearsed?'

'No. It was a total shock to me. I had no idea what he was going to say next. He just hijacked my routine and went raving on about that amoeba stuff, and I had to stand there like a dummy while everybody cracked up.'

'But, Jess, I'd never have guessed. You didn't even look surprised. I mean, you seemed to have lots of banter and . . .' Flora's voice trailed away.

'No!' snapped Jess. 'There was no *banter*! I managed to improvise a line or two – just to justify my existence, standing there like a lemon while he had the audience in stitches – but most of the material I'd worked on all week never got delivered. He stole the show – literally.'

'Wow!' Flora shook her head and ran her fingers through her long, honey-coloured hair in a gesture of bewilderment. 'I had no idea, babe. How awful for you!'

'So now maybe you understand,' concluded Jess bitterly, 'why I had to dump Fred.'

It was Sunday afternoon, the day after Chaos, the Valentine's dinner dance, and Jess had gone round to Flora's to talk it all through – because that's what best mates are for. Flora's dad had taken her mum out for Sunday lunch, her older sister Freya was away at Oxford and her younger sis Felicity was on an orchestra weekend, so Jess and Flora had the enormous cream sofa all to themselves.

'But you and Fred, you're just so obviously meant to be together!' Flora's huge blue eyes looked panicky and lost.

'I used to think that.' Jess shivered and snuggled more deeply under the elegant throw (100 per cent Italian cashmere, dove grey, no change from £300). 'But Fred was worse than useless even when he was trying to help. Basically, he pretended to be organising stuff and then later admitted he hadn't done anything! At the last minute, too! So *I* had to sort out the mess!'

'Chaos was a terrific success though. You made oodles of money for charity.'

'Only because my parents stepped in and sorted everything! I mean, we only had a band at all because my mum's boyfriend just happened to be a jazz musician and some of his mates just happened to be free.'

'But the band was great. And Martin seems a really nice guy.' Flora picked idly at some chocolate peanuts laid out on a porcelain dish on the coffee table. She

tended to nibble chocolatey things when stressed out
– who doesn't? 'Maybe he and your mum will become
an item, yeah? I mean, he could end up being your
stepdad.'

'I don't think so.' Jess shook her head doubtfully and
rested it against a satin cushion decorated with a trail of
tiny beads, like tears. 'Guess where Martin is right now?'

Flora shrugged and looked intrigued.

'On his way to Canada to have some kind of show-
down with his ex.'

'Oh no!' sighed Flora thoughtfully. 'Do you think
Mercury is retrograde or something? What else can
go wrong?'

'Plenty!' said Jess grimly.

Flora threw back her head and stared in disbelief at
the ceiling. A chandelier (Egyptian lead crystal
globes, no change from £400) sparkled above her
head and was reflected in her eyes. Jess noticed the
sparkle and gloomily compared the effect with her
own house, where dud light bulbs were often toler-
ated for weeks on end.

'But Fred . . .' sighed Flora, still staring at the twinkling chandelier. 'I mean, Fred . . . He's so original
and strange but somehow, you know, amazing. Why
don't you just freeze him out for a couple of days and

then, when he comes back on bended knee, you can make up again?'

Jess hesitated. A sudden uncomfortable thought had wormed its way into the far corner of her mind. Flora had fancied Fred once. She'd had the tiniest crush on him, just before Jess and Fred had got together. If Fred was apparently free and available now, might Flora be tempted to tempt him? Jess felt sick. She gulped hard.

'The thing is,' she confessed, 'I was thinking that if Fred wanted to get back together with me, he'd have to do something really major, like one of those medieval knights on a quest, you know?'

Flora frowned slightly. 'What do you mean?' she asked. 'Like, slay a dragon or something? Where's he going to find a dragon these days?'

'Slay a, well, a symbolic dragon, maybe.' Jess shrugged. The truth was, she wasn't exactly sure what she wanted Fred to do, but it just had to be massive to make up for all his recent spinelessness and selfishness. 'Oh, I don't know what – he'll have to think of something heroic.'

'Shall I . . . Would you like me to tell him that's what you want?' asked Flora, looking puzzled.

'No!' snapped Jess. She didn't want Flora as a

go-between: the dangers were obvious. 'I don't even want him to know that that's what I'm thinking. I want him to work it out for himself. I want him to realise what he's done and work out a way of putting it right.'

'But, babe,' persisted Flora uneasily, 'what if he gives up? All that heroic stuff, that doesn't really sound much like Fred, you know. What if he just goes back into his shell and mopes about miserably?'

'Well, if he reacts like that,' said Jess, horribly aware that Flora's scenario was all too likely, 'then my main job is to forget all about him – put him right out of my mind.'

Flora stared, speechless for a second. 'That's the plan?' she asked, looking less than convinced.

Jess nodded. 'Yes. Just get over him. I can't spend the rest of my life being let down by Fred. I'm going to wipe him clean out of my memory banks – starting from now.'

Flora sighed, leaning back against a sofa cushion and working her way through a whole handful of chocolate peanuts. 'This is so awful – I thought it was just a lovers' tiff. This is the worst thing that's happened for as long as I can remember.' She looked sombre.

'No need for gloom!' Jess was determined to change the mood to positive. 'This is the beginning of a brave new world, OK?'

Just then they heard Flora's front door being opened, in rather a rough and stressy manner, and then there was the alarming and unmistakable sound of Flora's mum running upstairs, crying.

Chapter 2

In the split second that followed, Jess and Flora just had time to lock eyes in sheer terror. Flora's mum *never* cried. She was the most laid-back mum in existence – so laid-back she barely ever left the sofa. What had happened? Death? Divorce? Cancer? Jess's mind reeled. But before she or Flora could utter even a frightened squeak, Flora's dad appeared in the doorway and the room went kind of dark.

He looked challenging, cross and deeply unhappy. Had Flora's parents had a row? Was a matrimonial breakdown looming?

'Right, Jess,' he said briskly.

Jess twitched in alarm to be singled out in this ominous way.

'If you're ready, I can give you a lift home now.'

Jess scrambled off the sofa obediently. 'Yes, right.

Thanks,' she muttered, stealing a furtive glance at Flora as she gathered up her fleece and bag.

Something bad had definitely happened. There never had been a plan for Mr Barclay to give her a lift home – she usually walked to and from Flora's. He'd obviously offered her a lift – or rather, forced one on her – as a polite way of getting her out of the house this instant.

'Bye then, Flo!' Jess leaned down and kissed Flora on the cheek. They briefly locked eyes in secret panic and then Jess had to turn away and walk out, smiling pleasantly as if nothing in the world was the matter, but knowing all the time that something awful was about to unfold in the Barclay house and there was nothing she could do to help.

Mr Barclay drove her home, slightly too fast, in his four-by-four. The silence was oppressive. Jess was so tempted to ask, 'Is Mrs Barclay OK?', but Mr Barclay's pursed lips suggested that small talk was forbidden. Jess had always been scared of Flora's dad. He was a big, powerful man who did deals and went on business trips to Italy, and he had no gift whatsoever for gentle chit-chat. Jess sat there dumbly waiting for the journey to end – preferably without a car crash.

Suddenly, out of the blue, her phone started to ring.

Mr Barclay sighed in exasperation, as if nobody had ever had the cheek to let their mobile ring in his presence before.

'Switch that off, please,' he growled.

Hastily Jess obeyed. She just had time to see that the caller ID showed Jodie from school, a bit-part player in Jess's circle of friends. Not Fred, then. Oh no! She wasn't supposed to be thinking about Fred, and the possibility of his calling her had made her heart give a tiny lurch. That must never happen again. Well, at least the call wasn't important – Jodie was always making some drama out of nothing.

Jess silently compared Mr Barclay to her own father, with his jolly jokes and occasional bouts of foolishness. How lucky she was to have a dad who talked so easily about silly things – about anything, in fact. She felt a huge pang of sympathy for Flora. Whenever Mr Barclay was in a stress about something, he seemed to emit black smoke. His bad moods were surely burning up the ozone layer.

Jess heaved a sigh – she couldn't help it – and hoped he hadn't heard it or interpreted it as some kind of impertinent challenge.

He reached across and switched on the radio. Some lovely gentle classical music filled the car. But that wasn't what he wanted: he twiddled the knobs until he found a sports commentary. It was motor racing, and its screaming crescendos blasted through Jess's brain until, mercifully, they arrived at her own little house.

'Thank you,' she said, flustered but trying to get out of the car in a relaxed and well-behaved manner.

Unfortunately the hem of her fleece got caught on the gearstick, the stretchy material holding her back as she tried to climb out, and when she yanked it free, the elastic catapulted the toggle right into her face. It hit her smartly on the nose.

'Ow!' gasped Jess.

Mr Barclay was watching the whole charade with an expression of the deepest contempt. Jess tried to find a wacky self-parodying smile.

'I'm such an idiot!' she sighed. He did not disagree. 'Thanks for the lift,' she concluded, nodding as if to confirm what a wonderful time they had had, and slammed the door shut. It didn't close properly. Jess tried to open it again, but it seemed locked. Mr Barclay frowned and rolled his eyes in a long-suffering way, reached across and opened the door himself from the inside. Jess got ready to slam it again, properly this time.

'Leave it! Leave it!' he snapped irritably. Jess leaped

back from the handle as if it was scalding hot. Mr Barclay slammed the door with furious panache, then grimly turned his eyes back to the road and drove off with an angry squeal of tyres.

'What an idiot!' muttered Jess under her breath.

She didn't like to be rude about Flora's dad, but really! He was such a weirdo – a bit like a robot. Most men have a feminine side if you look hard enough, but Mr Barclay ran on 100 per cent testosterone and even when things were going well and he might be expected to be happy, he somehow wore an expression of stressy responsibility and concern, like a tethered dog that's just waiting for a chance to bite somebody. Jess wondered briefly what he had been like as a boy. Nothing like Fred, that was for sure. Oh no! She had thought about Fred!

Jess wiped all thoughts of Fred from her mind, went up her own dear front path and entered her own dear house with relief. Luckily her mum was a peace-loving librarian who only ever cried in the happy bits of films, and then only quietly and furtively into her sleeve, with none of those hysterical sobs that had accompanied Mrs Barclay's strange charge upstairs.

Jess was grateful, too, for the benign influence of her granny who, though addicted to homicide on TV, could be relied upon to provide sensible and balanced insights into human behaviour. 'Tie him down and pour custard on his head!' had been her advice once when Jess had had an awful bust-up with Fred.

Above all, Jess was relieved that her dad was not an alpha-male control freak, but a gentle, gay painter of landscapes, who also cooked divinely and invented short stories in which magical things happened.

'I'm home!' called Jess.

There was no answer.

She poked her head into Granny's room – empty. She glanced into the kitchen – it was cold and tidy. She hauled herself upstairs and peeked into Mum's study – it was silent. The PC was switched off – there weren't even any electronic tropical fish wriggling their away across the screensaver to provide a friendly welcome.

Jess felt slightly annoyed, because she'd been bursting to tell everybody about the strange and awful way Mrs Barclay had run upstairs crying, and the horrendous lift home with Mr Barclay. It's all very well to have a wonderful family who have time to listen, and are chatty and gentle and supportive and all that jazz, but where were they when she needed them?

She slouched into her room and pulled up short.

Dad's stuff was all over the place – in organised piles, sure, but still kind of dominating what was her only private space in the world. She'd forgotten that Dad was using her room. Irritating. She trailed into the bedroom she was now sharing with her mum. Mum's clothes were all over the floor. Jess heaved a sigh. How could Mum be so messy? That was *her* job – she was the teenager, after all. And how many times had Mum told her off for being messy while herself creating total chaos whenever she was in a rush?

Jess placed her bag with ostentatious tidiness on the window sill, then slouched downstairs. She thought she might as well have a cup of hot chocolate (low-fat, naturally) because Sunday afternoons in February aren't famous for their riotous life-enhancing festivity and the day had been unexpectedly stressful. But before she could get anywhere with making it, she noticed a note on the table.

Jess, it read, in Mum's handwriting, *Fred's mum rang.*

Jess's heart lurched in alarm. Fred's mum? What was this? Holy moly! Fred . . . Fred dead? Heavens! Fred rhymed with dead! This was an omen! What was it about? Was there no message? Where was her own mum, just at the very moment Jess needed so desperately to interrogate her? Then she noticed another, smaller note in pencil.

Granny and I have gone to see the snowdrops at Stokebridge House.

Snowdrops! Honestly! Jess marvelled at the truly boring things which seemed to bring happiness to the older generations.

She loved Fred's mum: she was a cuddly, friendly, affectionate person, a bit like a living teddy bear. However, when unhappy, even she might be unexpectedly harsh. Jess was afraid that Fred's mum might have rung to give her a hard time about dumping Fred.

Jess hesitated, her heart racing. If the message had been *Fred rang*, she could have ignored it in a magnificently sulky way. It could have been part of the project to wipe Fred entirely from her memory banks. But she couldn't ignore Fred's mum. She prayed that Fred's mum wouldn't plead with her to make it up with Fred, or even murmur, tight-lipped, something about how upset she was that they'd parted. Jess crept reluctantly towards the phone as if it was a firework that hadn't gone off. Then, suddenly, it did go off – like the shrill cry of a wounded animal in the still, empty house.

Chapter 3

Jess picked up the receiver gingerly, as if it might be hot. Her mind was whirling. How should she be with Fred's mum? Sunny and friendly as if nothing was the matter? Polite but restrained?

'Hello?' she answered in a polite-but-restrained *and* sunny-and-friendly way. It was quite a strain on her hello but she wanted to cover all bases.

'Oh, Jess!' It was Flora. 'I've been calling your mobile but it's switched off!'

'Your dad told me to switch it off,' explained Jess, feeling guilty but somehow indignant at the same time.

'Honestly, he's such an idiot! He'll be back in a minute – I have to be quick. Listen, Jess, it's terrible. Apparently Dad's business is in serious trouble!'

'Really?' gasped Jess. Though she wasn't sure what this implied, it was certainly bad news.

'Yes!' Flora sounded distraught. 'Apparently the bottom's fallen out of the market!'

'How awful!' groaned Jess, trying to remember what Flora's dad actually did. She thought he sold bathrooms or something.

'My mum's still having a massive crying fit upstairs,' whispered Flora urgently. 'Dad's told her we might have to sell the house and move into somewhere much smaller!'

'Oh no, how awful!' sighed Jess sympathetically, even though she herself had always lived somewhere much smaller. 'Hey! Wait! The house next door to us is for sale – maybe you could move in there!' There was a tiny, icy pause.

'Oh, that would be lovely!' cried Flora. 'But we really need a four-bedroom house, right? Because there's three of us plus Mum and Dad.'

'Well, I'm sharing a bedroom with my freakin' mum at the moment,' Jess reminded her, 'because my dad's lost his meal ticket and his home in one insane moment of carelessness.'

'I know! What's happening to the world?' wailed Flora. 'Civilisation as we know it is breaking down! I might have to share a bedroom with Felicity so we can rent my room out! And Mum's got to try and find a job – it's a disaster!'

'My dad's looking for work, too,' Jess reminded her. She felt sorry for Flora, but she didn't feel the Barclay family had an absolute monopoly on bad news.

'I've got to go now, babe. I can hear Dad's car – he's going to have to sell that, too. Apparently we might not be able to afford a car at all, or if we can afford one it'll be tiny!'

'That's so harsh!' cried Jess, whose mum's car was so old, it had once been pulled by horses. 'Flo, I'm so, so sorry for you!' she assured her, fighting back her uncharitable thoughts.

'Got to go. Let's talk later!' Flora hissed, and then she was gone.

Jess replaced the phone and stared at the wall. Poor Flora! She'd always had a privileged lifestyle, with trips to the Caribbean, chandeliers and cashmere throws, and a lovely lazy mum who drifted around the house in negligees and spent her time planning treats for herself and others. Jess had never been *really* jealous because she liked her own little house and her mum and granny, and the atmosphere at Flora's elegant house was often much more stressy.

She reflected, with a tiny sliver of satisfaction, that

Flora would now have to find out what it was like to be hard up – like Jess herself, whose mum was a librarian and whose granny lived on a pension. Librarians aren't famous for their chandeliers. You don't see librarians posing on the red carpet at premieres, dripping with diamonds and all decked out in designer wear.

Jess sighed. Though she felt real sympathy for Flora, and was shocked that this had happened, there seemed to be so many other complicated thoughts flooding through her mind. *Maybe*, suggested some small, questioning part of her mind, *it won't be such a bad thing for Flora to find out what life is like in the real world*. But as it seemed rather mean to have such a thought in the middle of a crisis like this, Jess tried to suppress it, and began to wonder if she was suffering from low blood sugar since her thoughts seemed so muddled. She and Flora had only had a meagre salad for lunch because they'd decided they were both getting porky. Jess would have to fix herself a sandwich.

Then her eye fell on the message again: *Jess, Fred's mum rang*. Help! That other crisis! The massive, life-changing one!

Should she ring right away or have a sandwich first? In a way, Jess just wanted to get it over with, so she grabbed the phone again and dialled Fred's landline. It was always possible that Fred himself would answer it, so she cleared her throat nervously and prepared a frosty but friendly act to greet him with when he picked up.

'Hello?' It was Fred's mum.

'Hello, Mrs Parsons. This is Jess.'

'Oh, Jess! Well done on having such a success last night with Chaos! Peter said it was packed out and there was a terrific atmosphere.'

Who was Peter? Oh yes! Fred's dad, who had organised the bar.

'It was really kind of Mr Parsons to help us out with the bar,' said Jess. She couldn't believe Fred's mum had called earlier just to congratulate her on her dinner dance.

'I'm just sorry I couldn't have been there,' Mrs Parsons went on. 'But as Fred's probably told you, my mother's got this flu bug.'

'Oh no! I'm sorry to hear that!' cried Jess. 'Fred didn't mention it.'

'I think she must have caught it off Fred,' Mrs Parsons rabbited on. 'She's quite ill with it, so I've been spending a lot of time round at her flat. It's been quite a week, having Fred laid up here and Mum on the other side of town.'

'You poor thing!' Jess wondered where this conversation was going.

'Poor Fred's had a bit of a relapse,' Mrs Parsons went on.

'Oh no!' exclaimed Jess, feeling a lurch of alarm, and then swallowing it and trying to remind herself that it served him right for snatching the limelight and forcing her to abandon her stand-up routine while he pranced around dressed like an amoeba – the *idiot*.

'I don't think he was quite well enough to go to the dinner dance last night,' Mrs Parsons went on, 'but he insisted he was OK – he obviously didn't want to let you down.'

He didn't want to let her down? He'd done nothing but let her down for weeks and weeks while she was desperately trying to organise the wretched thing! What Jess longed to say now was: '*He didn't want to miss an opportunity to grab the limelight and steal the show, you mean!*' But Mrs Parsons didn't have a clue what had really happened at Chaos and Jess knew that people can get a bit uncomfortable if you criticise their children, so she was forced to soft-pedal.

'I wasn't expecting Fred to turn up, in fact,' she protested, trying to sound relaxed about the whole thing, though she was actually about as relaxed as a water-hating bulldog in a bathtub full of bubbles. 'I would've managed OK on my own. It really wasn't necessary for Fred to come.'

'Oh, he wouldn't have wanted to let you down,' Mrs Parsons repeated in a sentimental, hero-worshipping kind of voice which Jess found deeply irritating. 'He would've known how much it meant to you to have his support.' Jess was obviously supposed to join in the praise of St Fred at this point, assuring his mum that life without him was impossible, hollow and meaningless.

'What a shame he made himself ill, though,' Jess went on briskly. 'Will he have to miss school tomorrow?'

'Probably – he's gone back to bed and he's got a temperature again,' said his mum dolefully. 'He mentioned that Stephen King book he lent you – maybe you could drop it in tomorrow on your way back from school?'

'OK, fine,' said Jess. She would have to ask Mackenzie to drop off the book instead. The last thing she wanted was a near-deathbed reunion with Fred – or even a near-deathbed row. They'd had rows at Fred's house before, and as the walls were quite thin they'd had to whisper their insults, which had been a shame – there really is no substitute, at such times, for demented yelling.

'Oh, I've got to go now,' said Fred's mum. 'He's calling.' She paused, obviously waiting for Jess to say '*Give him my love*' or something similarly tender and loving.

'OK.' Jess moved swiftly away from romance. 'Thank Mr Parsons again for helping us out – it was really great of him.'

Seconds after Jess put the phone down, as she was heading for the fridge and salivating for England, the wretched thing rang again.

'Jess, this is your useless dad.' There was traffic noise in the background. 'I've broken down on the A40 on the way to Oxford, and my mobile's out of charge. I need you to ring Jim and the people who rented me this van.'

'Who? What?'

'First ring Jim, the guy who loaned us the lights. I'm taking them back to him, remember? I need you to find his number. It's in my address book, which I think is in the top left-hand pocket of my jacket, which might be hanging on the back of your bedroom door. No, uhhh – it might be in the back pocket of my jeans, which are folded up in my suitcase. No, wait – it might be in that computer bag . . .'

Jess felt as if she was being enveloped by fog. What else could go wrong?

Chapter 4

Next morning, Jess spent an extra ten minutes on her eyebrows. Telling everyone at school that she and Fred were finished was going to be a big cringe, and she wanted to look her best even though Fred wouldn't be there himself. Somehow Fred getting ill again was almost too convenient because all the embarrassing stuff of telling people it was over had to be done by Jess. As usual, he had dumped the chores on her. But first she had to get through the breakfast performance – it had become a performance since Dad moved in. He was definitely a morning person.

'Right!' said Dad, rubbing his hands. 'How about scrambled eggs, bacon, tomatoes, sausages, beans and fried potatoes? That'll set you up for a day of strenuous skiving!'

Mum was loading the dishwasher with last night's

dirty plates and Granny was nowhere to be seen –
having a lie-in, evidently. Mum glanced anxiously at
the clock. 'Tim, Jess has to leave in five minutes and
I have to leave in ten, so shall we save the big food
event for tonight? And don't forget I have high
cholesterol.'

'Yeah, Dad. Don't be upset. It's not that we don't
love the idea of your scrummy feast.' Jess squeezed
his arm. 'It's just that I usually only have a slice of
toast nowadays.'

'Jambalaya!' cried Dad boisterously.

'What?' asked Jess, urgently looking for her French
coursework book in the vegetable box.

'Jambal . . . aya!' repeated Dad, singing it as if it was
part of a comic opera. 'It's a Cajun dish with the same
ingredients as the traditional English breakfast: scrambled eggs, sausages . . .'

'Tim,' said Mum seriously, 'I really appreciate your
cooking, but could we please have some low-fat, low-
cholesterol dishes? Salmon fillets or something? And
maybe broccoli?'

'I hate the smell of broccoli cooking!' said Dad with
a grin. 'It smells like an aardvark farting!'

Mum gave him a disgusted glance. 'You seem to be
in high spirits,' she observed icily. 'What's your plan

of action for today? If you have any spare time you can get the groceries.' She pushed a list across the table. 'It would save me having to nip out of the library at lunchtime.'

'Consider it done!' cried Dad with an exaggerated flourish of the arm. 'Today is the first day of the rest of my life. I realised last night that finishing with Phil is the liberation I've needed for ages!' Dad was camping out in Jess's room because he'd been dumped by his previously divine partner, Phil. It seemed to be dumping season.

'Being liberated into poverty, you mean?' asked Mum ironically.

'Well, in a way, yes!' Dad looked positively delighted at the prospect of being penniless. 'I shouldn't have let him support me like that financially. I should have been out supporting myself.'

'And us?' remarked Mum with a sarcastic lift of the eyebrow.

'Yes, yes! You, too! I'm going to live responsibly from now on. I'm going to go out and get a proper job today, and then I'm going to find somewhere to live so I'll be out of your hair by – oh, the end of the week, probably.'

'Well, I'll believe it when it happens,' commented Mum drily.

'Give Dad a break!' protested Jess. She knew it must be weird for her parents to be sharing a house, even temporarily, after spending the past fourteen years apart, but she didn't like the way Mum was sneering at Dad's brave new start in life.

'OK, OK! I'm just a bit grumpy this morning,' said Mum, with the faintest hint of a smile. She was so not a morning person. 'Because it's Monday, I expect. I'm glad you feel liberated, Tim, though we did like Phil. I expect you'll find it liberating, too, love,' she added, turning to Jess, 'not going out with Fred any more.' Mum looked a bit uncertain and slightly awkward.

'What?' cried Dad in surprise. 'You've finished with Fred? Nobody told me! When did this happen?'

'You were busy all yesterday,' said Jess, diving speedily into her coat. 'Driving to Oxford and stuff.' She didn't want this conversation right now.

'But why?' wailed Dad in dismay. 'The lad is perfect for you – perfect!'

'Not now, Dad. I'll tell you all about it tonight, OK?' Jess escaped out of the kitchen and headed for the door.

'Take your fur-trapper's hat!' called Mum. 'It's going to be freezing today! And take a banana!'

Jess grabbed a banana, took her hat down off the peg in the hall and put her head round Granny's door to say goodbye. Granny was sitting up in bed, drinking tea and watching the news on TV.

'They've found a girl who disappeared twenty years ago,' Granny reported breathlessly. 'Her family thought she'd been murdered but she was just locked in a shed in some backyard.'

'Great news, Granny!' beamed Jess. She kissed Granny on the cheek and then set off hastily for school as she was already late.

As she walked along the frosty pavements she thought how ironic it was that it was 'good' news that a girl had *only* been kidnapped for twenty years. So there were people worse off than herself – she must remember that.

As she trudged, her school bag bounced heavily against her back. Fred's wretched Stephen King habit! She'd never managed to get into that kind of book, preferring not to read about strange and fatal goings-on (she hadn't inherited Granny's murder addiction), but Fred kept lending her these books the size of bricks and insisting that they were amazing and mind-blowing. Well, they certainly were back-blowing – she'd be black and blue by the time she got to school.

She arrived to find the bell had gone for registration, but when she reached the classroom, Mr Fothergill hadn't arrived, so everyone was just sitting around chatting.

'Hey, Jess!' Jodie screeched across the room. 'Is it true you've dumped Fred? Or did he dump you?'

Jess felt a wave of shock and horror. She'd been planning to hint what had happened between her and Fred, very quietly and subtly, to a few select friends at lunchtime. Instead, the news was being bellowed out over the whole county by the girl with the loudest voice in the world.

Who had told her? Flora was sitting beside Jodie, looking guilty. Jess gave them a withering glare. OK, she hadn't actually asked Flo not to mention it, and everybody had to be told somehow or other, but to have it blasted out all over the school like this . . . !

Jess ignored Jodie and went to sit beside Mackenzie and Pete Collins, a boy with buck-teeth, large ears and a happy grin.

'Hi, Mackenzie,' she said. 'How's it going?'

'Great stand-up routine the other night,' he said. 'I reckon you and Fred should go to the Edinburgh Festival this summer – I was going to offer to set it all up for you.' Mackenzie fancied himself as a bit of an impresario. 'But is that true, what Jodie just said? You haven't actually dumped Fred, the comedy legend?'

Jess could see Jodie heading towards them, accompanied by the screech and clatter of furniture that had inconveniently got in her way. Swiftly Jess pulled the Stephen King book out of her school bag.

'Well, Fred and I aren't best buddies any more,' she murmured to Mackenzie. 'In fact, I was wondering if you could drop this at his place on your way home from school? Apparently Fred's flu has come back and he won't be in today.'

Mackenzie seemed to hesitate. He took the book in his hand and pursed his lips in doubtful style. 'Actually, I was going to watch BJ in a football match right after school,' he said. 'We're playing Fernlea.'

Jodie's determined paw swiped the book right out of Mackenzie's hesitating hand. 'I'll take it to Fred's,' she announced firmly.

Jess felt a spear of furious indignation slice through her heart, but she couldn't find the words which would express her feelings of outrage. She hastily tried to compose herself and retain her dignity – after all, she was trying to create the impression of somebody totally in control of her life and feelings. Nobody must know how much Fred had hurt her or how disturbed she was by the thought of him not being her boyfriend any more. So she confined herself to giving Jodie a scorching look that could have grilled bacon.

'What?' demanded Jodie, cocking her head on one side with barefaced confidence. 'I pass his house on my way home. Anyway, if you've dumped him, somebody's got to call in and cheer him up, right?'

Chapter 5

Jess got her first chance for a word alone with Flora at break.

'Why did you have to tell Jodie?' she demanded. Flora twitched and looked guilty.

'I'm sorry, babe,' she whispered. 'I didn't know it was meant to be a secret.'

'Well,' Jess hesitated, 'OK. It can't be a secret – people have to know – but Jodie yelling across the classroom like that! It was so utterly cringeworthy.'

'I'm sorry,' repeated Flora, and her big blue eyes filled up with tears.

Jess squeezed her arm. 'Hey!' she murmured gently. 'No need to get upset about it! It doesn't matter.'

'It's just . . . I feel a bit weird today,' gulped Flora.

'Let's get some chocolate bars!' suggested Jess, steering Flora in the direction of the tuck shop.

'No, no,' sighed Flora. 'I don't want to go down that road. It's just, you know . . .' She sat down on a low wall that ran along the edge of the school's quad. 'I feel kind of wobbly . . . Apparently Mum's thinking of doing Bed and Breakfast, and I'll have to give up my bedroom because it's en suite.'

'Oh no!' exclaimed Jess. 'Harsh!' She didn't mention the fact that she had never had an en-suite bedroom and that hadn't ruined her life, so doing without one wasn't going to ruin Flora's.

'Mum's gone ballistic . . .' Flora hesitated. 'It's because my dad's known about the situation for some time, but he didn't tell her. He couldn't face it. So she was completely in the dark.'

'Why didn't he tell her?'

'Well, my dad kind of worships my mum. I know he seems a bit of an ogre and he's always so confident and everything, but he really puts her up on a pedestal. He calls her Princess. He wants to protect her from bad things and look after her and everything – you know, like a "good provider". He never wanted her to have to go out to work, but now she will have to. She was crying all night.'

'My mum's always had to go out to work!' observed Jess sharply.

Flora looked startled for a split second, then recovered herself. 'Oh yeah, I know. It'll be totally good for Mum and stuff. In fact, she was saying so this morning at breakfast. I hate seeing my mum cry, though – it's really disturbing.'

'Yeah, of course.' Jess tried to think of something comforting to say. 'I think having a job has kept my mum sane, you know – and she feels kind of confident because of it. Maybe your mum could get a job at the library! I'll ask Mum if there are any vacancies.'

'Thanks,' said Flora wanly. She didn't look very hopeful. 'The trouble is, Dad says, there's so much unemployment at the moment that for every job Mum applies for, there are also loads of young graduates applying.' She sighed again. 'That's why B & B seems like the only option.'

'Hey! That girl over there looks a bit like a duck,' whispered Jess, trying to distract Flora with random comedy.

Flora regarded the girl thoughtfully. She didn't smile. 'I can't bear the thought of having to share a bedroom with Felicity.' She pulled a disgusted face. 'She spends hours every evening tootling away on her stupid flute, for a start.'

'Well . . .' Jess was trying her hardest to give Flora

some perspective. 'Right now, remember, I'm sharing with my actual *mum*, because my useless dad is camping out in my bedroom.'

'Yes, but it's not so bad for you,' said Flora sadly.

'Why not so bad?'

'You're used to . . .' Flora appeared to change her mind about what to say and blushed slightly. 'Your family is so much more – kind of flexible.'

Jess felt a surge of fiery annoyance. She knew what Flora was really thinking and she was dissing her house! 'Yeah,' she said crisply. 'It's been hard, living in a hovel, but I guess we peasants have never known anything better.'

Flora turned to Jess with a frantic, panicky stare and grabbed Jess's sleeve. 'Babe, I didn't mean . . . I mean, I'm sorry, I'm talking garbage. It's just that you're so much better off than me. *Really!*'

'How?' Jess was genuinely puzzled.

'Because your parents . . . They're already divorced!'

'You don't mean your . . . ?'

Flora shrugged. 'Who knows? The way Mum was talking last night, she . . . It's been such a shock, I don't know . . . She can be impulsive.'

Jess was silent, trying to imagine what it was like to have an impulsive mother. She often wished her mum was more impulsive and not so careful all the time. OK, Mum had done a bit of internet dating recently, which admittedly was quite impulsive, but she'd gone about it in an ultra-careful way, even dragging Jess along on some dates just to avoid being alone with strange guys.

'And anyway . . .' Flora resumed her train of thought. 'You're only sharing your mum's room for a few days till your dad finds somewhere of his own, right? I'll be sharing with Felicity, like, *for ever.*'

'What happens when Freya comes home from Oxford?' asked Jess, trying to imagine the glamorous and extravagant Freya fitting into the Barclays' nouveau-poor lifestyle.

'Once Freya gets her head round all this,' said Flora ominously, 'I don't think she ever *will* come home from Oxford.'

There was a silence as a gang of younger kids walked past on their way to gym.

'But never mind all that,' said Flora eventually. 'What about Jodie going round to Fred's? How can we stop her?'

'Why should we stop her?' shrugged Jess. 'It's a free country.'

'You mean you don't mind her going round to see Fred?'

Jess considered for a minute or four. Thoughts and feelings were whirling around in her brain like random garments in a tumble-dryer: murderous rage, homicidal rage, speechless rage, quivering rage . . .

'Oh, I don't care,' she said. 'After all, Fred and I are finished, so he's free to do what he wants, isn't he?'

It wasn't so much Jodie going to see Fred in her usual barging, blundering way that bothered Jess – what really mattered was Fred's reaction. If Fred really cared for Jess, surely he would be hurt that she hadn't brought the book round herself. Maybe he had asked his mum for the Stephen King book deliberately, to engineer a visit from Jess . . . But on the other hand, their relationship wasn't going to be put right by Jess making the moves and making all the effort. She still felt stung by his bad behaviour, and he was going to have to go out of his way and take the initiative to patch things up, not summon her to his bedside like a servant.

Next morning Jess got to school early and she and Flora bagged the best radiator.

'What's the latest on the home front?' whispered Jess.

'Oh, Mum's really getting into this B & B thing now,' said Flora. 'She loves a project, you know.

Apparently I can have Freya's room while she's away at uni.' So Flora wasn't going to have to share with Felicity after all – most of the time.

'How do you feel about it now?' asked Jess.

Flora shrugged. 'There's so much else going on. Dad was in a weird mood last night. He said we should move to Australia.'

Jess grabbed Flora's arm. 'No way am I going to let them drag you off there!' she cried in alarm. 'Unless I can come with you! Hey! Maybe that's the answer! Imagine the surfing! The bronzed lifeguards!'

'Mum said no,' Flora went on. 'She said it would ruin her skin. So he backed down. But he still looks weird, as if he might do something unpredictable. Mum hid his car keys this morning because she was afraid he'd go and drive off a cliff somewhere.'

Jess stared in astonishment. She couldn't imagine her own dad driving off a cliff – he got vertigo on the escalators in the mall.

'It's his masculine pride, I suppose,' added Flora.

'I don't think my dad has got any masculine pride,' said Jess. 'He was even talking last night about getting a job as a carer.'

Flora looked surprised. 'I can't imagine my dad doing that,' she mused.

Then, suddenly, Jodie appeared. She headed straight for them.

'Fred's getting better,' she reported. 'His mum says she thinks he'll be well enough to come back to school tomorrow.' She stared at Jess in a curious, challenging way.

Fred's mum had been talking to Jodie, just like she normally talked to Jess! But why shouldn't she?

'We played Scrabble,' Jodie went on, plonking herself down in a chair and chucking her bag on the floor. 'Fred scored two hundred and sixty and I scored ninety-six. He said I had a brain the size of a pea! Ha, ha!'

Jess smelled danger. OK, to an ignorant outsider it might sound as if Fred was dissing Jodie, but Jess knew that was the way Fred delivered his compliments. A cold wave of anxiety washed over her. Bravely she struggled to ignore it. So Fred and Jodie had played Scrabble? So what? So that must have lasted at least an hour, if not an hour and a half. That was what. And he'd said she had a brain the size of a pea – he was showering her with compliments. In Jess's fevered imagination, Fred and Jodie were already an item.

Chapter 6

In fact, it was two days before Fred put in an appearance at school. The circumstances weren't ideal. Jess had overslept and arrived late, just as Mr Fothergill was finishing taking the register. She didn't see Fred, sitting at the back – everybody was just a blur. She'd had to run part of the way and she knew her face was as red as a sunset in Red Square.

'Sorry, Mr Fothergill,' she puffed. 'My dad's car wouldn't start so I had to walk.' This was a double lie. Her dad didn't even have a bicycle, let alone a car.

Fothers peered at her over the top of his glasses. 'If you're late one more time, Jess Jordan,' he said, trying to be stern, 'I shall have to take serious disciplinary action.'

'I promise it won't happen again,' Jess assured him.

Old Fothers couldn't dish out the strict stuff – he was about as threatening as a toy koala. But Mr Powell (Irritable Powell to his victims), Head of Year, well, he had a shout that could split seasoned oak logs – he could get a weekend job at the sawmill.

Jess flashed a dazzling smile at Mr Fothergill. She knew she was one of his favourites. Old Fothers was a bit inclined to showbiz – in another life he might have been a TV comedian – and he liked Jess because of her comedy ambitions.

'Sit down,' growled Mr Fothergill, trying to be severe. He scratched his head distractedly and somehow his glasses dropped off his face.

There were a few titters from the room.

Jess escaped towards the back of the class, and it was at this point that she saw Fred. The only free seat was across the aisle from him so she had to sit there. It was too late to ignore him – she had already locked eyes with him and as the shock jolted her ribcage, she could feel a huge, blazing blush spreading right over her face.

At this point Joe Kennedy went up to ask Mr Fothergill something, and while they were talking, a quiet buzz of discussion spread through the class. Jess sat down and wondered whether she should turn and say hello to Fred. After all, they couldn't just ignore each other. *That* would be stupid. No, she wouldn't look at him. He would have to make the first move.

'Hey!' she heard Fred's voice, softly, from across the aisle, and had turned her head before she'd even had time to decide if it would be a good idea or not. He was looking quizzically at her. 'I think I recognise you,' said Fred. 'You used to be Jess Jordan, didn't you?'

Jess felt stung, even though this wasn't a direct insult – it was a weird thing to say and hinted at their break-up in public. Aware that people nearby were eavesdropping and sniggering, she had to think of a stinging retort.

'I don't recognise you, though.' She frowned. 'Oh, wait. I think I did see you once before – when I was looking down a microscope.'

There were more giggles and Jess turned away to her left. She felt she had scored a point against Fred, but somehow it had secretly hurt *her*.

Beatrice Ashton was sitting next to her, looking rather like a worried meerkat. She had a long pointy nose, big soft anxious eyes and short furry hair. The only thing missing was the tail.

'Hi, Beatrice!' beamed Jess. She'd never taken much notice of Beatrice before, but now that she was determinedly ignoring Fred, she and Beatrice would have to get on. 'How's it going?'

Disastrously, Beatrice's eyes filled with tears. 'My mum's got to go into hospital to have a hysterectomy!' she wailed. 'And dad says that the hospital's got a terrible record with infections and stuff! I was looking on the internet last night and I read about all these flesh-eating bugs that can literally eat up your whole body!'

Jess shuddered in horror and laid a sympathetic hand on Beatrice's arm. She had to reassure her. 'I'm sure your mum will be OK,' she said. 'My mum had a hysterectomy in St George's two years ago and she was fine. In fact, she was playing tennis again after a few weeks.'

Beatrice's eyes grew large with amazement. 'Really?' she breathed.

Jess nodded. 'Really!' she assured her.

Please God, she added in a silent prayer, *forgive me for lying about my mum – she's never indulged in tennis or hysterectomies, as thou knowest, but I had to cheer poor Bea up somehow.*

'Oh thanks!' Beatrice gasped, squeezing Jess's hand. 'Would it be OK if my mum rang your mum up just to, like, talk it through with her?'

'Of course!' Jess agreed, panicking in the invisible

depths of her heart. Despite her very prompt apology to God, she was now up to her eyebrows in the smelly stuff. She scribbled a phone number down on a piece of paper and gave it to Beatrice. It wasn't Jess's land-line number – in fact, it was a random stream of digits, but Jess had to buy some time.

'I didn't sleep a wink last night!' confided Beatrice. 'I didn't dare to, because the night before I had a dream that Mum died!'

Ease up, Bea, thought Jess irritably. *When I asked how it was going, I wasn't offering counselling.* Jess was distracted by the sound of Fred saying something, but Bea's up-close nervous breakdown had obliterated the details. There was a ripple of laughter. Fred had said something funny! What was it? What if it was about her?

Jess felt awful for fixating on what Fred might be saying behind her back when she knew that it was her duty as a human being to comfort Bea in her hour of need. And she was genuinely grateful that her own mum wasn't scheduled for major surgery or about to be eaten alive by a rampant bacterium, but still, she wished she'd never got into all this.

When Jess had asked Bea 'How's it going?' the correct reply was so obviously 'Great, thanks. How are *you*?'. Bea had broken all the rules by ranting on about her drama and Jess had been punished for these horrid thoughts. It would only be a matter of time before Bea located Jess's real phone number and telephoned to interrogate her mum about an op she had never even had. Worst of all, Jess had nobody to blame for this debacle but herself.

'Right!' said Mr Fothergill, as a shrill bell rang out, summoning the innocent victims to double maths – always such a pleasure. 'Off you go!'

'Don't worry, Bea. It'll be all right!' hissed Jess, shooting out of her chair like a sprinter out of the blocks and heading for the door. No way was she going to be recruited as Bea's substitute best friend while Emma Forrester was away (with earache, presumably). Jess wasn't going to hang about anyway – she didn't want to look needy or as if she was half-hoping Fred would walk with her or offer her some charming compliment. She wasn't even going to wait for Flora. She simply hurtled towards Double Maths as eagerly as if it was a pizza parlour with a 'buy one get one free' evening.

At lunchtime it was raining so hard, the ~~~ing school yard had become a white-water rafting Jess and Flora headed for the form r number of cosy activities was taking place: gossip, DIY felt-tip tattooing, drawing moustaches on photos of glamorous female celebs in a gossip magazine. In a far corner Fred appeared to be playing chess with Mackenzie – watched by Jodie. Despite the fact that there were twenty-three other people present and literally dozens of things going on, the minute Jess entered the room she saw that Jodie's left hand was resting on the back of Fred's chair and that her finger-tips were touching his back – or, if not actually touching, were near enough to feel his aura.

Having been sliced in half by that agonising sight, Jess headed for the opposite corner of the room, an expression of gaiety nailed to her face. At least Beatrice didn't seem to be around – that was some comfort – though Jess hoped guiltily that she wasn't weeping in the toilets.

Having bagged a radiator, Jess and Flora formed a very private conversation space and Flora whipped out a pack of chocolate animals.

'Chocolate is OK after all,' she whispered, offering Jess one. 'Scientists have found it contains something or other that's good for you.'

Jess took an elephant and rammed it in her mouth. 'At times like this,' she said, 'only chocolate will keep me sane. These animals are so endangered, they won't be here in two minutes' time.'

'What have you got to worry about?' asked Flora challengingly. 'I'm being turfed out of my room, my mum and dad are rowing for England and we've had to cancel our Easter trip to Barbados.'

At this point there was an explosion of cheering in the chess-playing corner. Fred had evidently beaten Mackenzie because he was punching the air. His long thin arms, which had so often been nicely wrapped around Jess, now seemed disturbingly distant and free-range.

'RE-SULT!' yelled Jodie, and thumped him on the back. 'Hey, everybody! There's a chess match against St Patrick's tonight, so we've all got to stay after school and support Fred!'

'What?' asked Jess with a sudden burst of irritation. 'Cheering on the sidelines after every move? Sorry, I forgot my ra-ra skirt and pom-poms.'

'You've got to come, Jess!' Jodie went on relentlessly. 'Everybody's going!'

If Jodie was going to stage-manage Fred's fan club, that was one organisation Jess would never join.

'I can't, sorry,' Jess said quickly. 'I'm busy after school.'

'Doing what?' demanded Jodie.

'Mind your own business!' snapped Jess. It sounded stupid and stressy, and she was aware that the chess match against St Patrick's might be a lot of fun with everybody there. She was also aware that Fred would look very charming, as he always did when he was concentrating on something, with a cute serious frown and his eyes very big and grey and thoughtful, and she was going to miss it all, and that she had nobody to blame but herself.

Chapter 7

After school Jess and Flora called in at the Dolphin Cafe. It was packed, so they had to sit on a couple of stools facing the wall. Jess had a latte, but Flora was drinking water – partly to be healthy and partly to try and save money.

'I've got into this Being Poor business now,' she said.

Jess sipped her latte, feeling a bit guilty. Should she have insisted on buying Flora a latte, too?

'I'm going to sell all my old clothes on eBay,' Flora went on. 'Plus I'm looking for a Saturday job. Hey! Maybe we could look for one together!'

'Yeah, why not?' Jess nodded. Secretly, she could think of nothing worse. The whole point about Saturdays was being able to have a bit of a lie-in, and then, having crawled out of bed around noon, to survey the hours and hours of delicious free time ahead. She didn't want to say so, though. It was important to give Flo as much support as possible.

'We could clean cars in the supermarket car park,' Flora mused. 'Some people were doing it last week. They had a bucket full of money.'

'I think that was for charity, though,' said Jess. 'We could hardly say, "*We're cleaning cars in aid of our fat and pampered selves.*"'

'Yes, I am horribly porky,' lamented Flora, whose tum was in reality so flat that if she was lying down you could have used her as a coffee table.

Jess sighed. 'I didn't mean you, dummy,' she said, grinning reproachfully. Then she sighed again. 'I wonder how the chess is going?' she murmured.

'Why didn't you go?' asked Flora.

'What? Sit there and watch Jodie drooling all over Fred? I'd rather eat a whole stupid chess set, including the board.'

'Of course!' Flora sympathised. 'But you'll soon be back together again, won't you? Once Fred has performed his heroic task and got himself back into your good books. Are you sure you don't want me to have a word with him about it?'

'No!' snapped Jess.

She had enough to worry about with Jodie circling

around Fred. The last thing she needed now was Flora arranging intimate little chats with him. Apart from Flora's dodgy history of fascination with Fred, Jess didn't see why Flo should have the pleasure of his company. Although it was only a couple of days since they'd split up, she missed being with him. It was torment, thinking of him cracking jokes for other people. With any luck, it was torment for him, too, not having her at his side. Or was he happy to act the clown for just about anybody?

'I hate all this breaking-up stuff,' said Flora miserably. 'My parents are still rowing all the time about Dad's business probs.'

'Blaming each other?' asked Jess.

'No, it's quite sweet in a way. Both of them are determined to blame themselves. Dad's, like, "I invested way too much when the economic situation was already a bit iffy. I should have seen the signs and downsized much earlier. I've let you down, Princess." And then Mum says, "No, no, it's all my fault! I've been so lazy all these years, just messing about at home. If I'd got myself off the sofa and found a job, we wouldn't be in the pickle we're in now."'

'That doesn't sound like a row to me,' said Jess doubtfully. 'When Mum and I have a row there's a lot of yelling and once I even threw a plate at her.'

'Did you, babe? Wow! You smashed china?'

'Well, actually it was a plastic plate,' confessed Jess. 'And it missed her by a mile and bounced harmlessly off the wall. So we're not much good at having rows, either. Although the atmosphere at home is a bit tense right now because Dad's under Mum's feet all the time.'

'Isn't that nice, though – to be all together as a family for a while?'

'It might be, if we had a spare room,' grumbled Jess.

Flora nodded, then her eyes took on a rather gloomy, faraway look. 'Mercury really must be retrograde or something.'

'Cheer up!' said Jess. 'We can always have little treats – go to the movies or something.'

'If I can afford it,' sighed Flora, heading for another blue mood.

When Jess got home there was a delicious cheesy smell – Granny was bustling about in the kitchen.

'What's that divine smell, you culinary genius?' Jess gave Granny a big hug.

She realised how lucky she was. She had relatively healthy parents (touch wood, thank goodness, etc.), plus it was apparently an advantage that they were amicably divorced. Best of all, she had a granny who was loving, active and only interested in murder as a spectator rather than as a participant.

'It's that cheese and potato pie thing I make sometimes,' said Granny. 'I made it to cheer your mum up. She's a bit down. I told her to go up and have a nice hot bath.'

'What's wrong with Mum, then?' asked Jess, flinging her school bag into the corner of the kitchen which, in more civilised households, would have held a dog basket containing a divine little poodle called Doodle.

'Well, just after she'd got home from work, the phone rang!' Granny leaned forward and dropped her voice to a confidential whisper, even though Mum, upstairs in the bathroom with both taps running and the radio on, was as likely to hear this conversation as she was to appreciate the distant sounds of a piano recital in New York's Carnegie Hall. 'It was that Martin!' Granny went on. 'I never much liked him!'

Oh no! Mum's first decent date since the break-up with Dad – not counting last year's Japanese toy boy.

'What's happened to Martin?' asked Jess fearfully.

'Well, you know he went off to Canada to see his ex and he told your mum he was going to "sort everything out"? And she assumed, of course, that he meant he was going to finalise his separation, maybe arrange a divorce and so on. Well, the opposite has happened! It's all on again with his ex, apparently. In fact, he's applying for a job in Canada – as a music teacher.'

'What a shame,' said Jess. 'I really liked him. Although now, of course, I never want to see him again.'

'Well, dear,' said Granny briskly. 'I've heard there are terrible mosquitoes in Canada, so . . .' She winked roguishly.

'I suppose that's some comfort,' said Jess, nodding. She felt really sorry for Mum, but she hoped there wouldn't be any heartbroken moping. That kind of thing isn't very attractive in the middle-aged. 'Oh well,' she went on. 'That's enough bad news for one evening, Granny. Fingers crossed nothing else bad will happen and we can do our best to cheer Mum up. I vote we light a log fire and blow the dust off the DVD of *Some Like It Hot*.'

At this point the phone rang. A tiny, stupid part of Jess's brain insisted on thinking it might be Fred, even though she was 95 per cent sure he was still playing chess, or possibly eating jam tarts and quaffing celebratory champagne round at Jodie's. She grabbed the phone anyway.

'Hello?' she said sweetly.

'Mrs Jordan?' It was a woman's voice. 'This is Sarah Ashton, Beatrice's mother. Bea's in Jess's class. Jess told her today that you'd had a hysterectomy and you wouldn't mind telling me about it. My op is scheduled for next week, you see, and I'm getting myself in a state about it. I hope you don't mind me ringing? The number Jess gave Bea didn't work so we looked you up in the phone book.'

Chapter 8

Jess had a five-second nervous breakdown. What to do? Pretend it was a wrong number? But the Ashtons had just looked it up in the phone book. Pretend her mum was out? But that would only postpone all kinds of awful hassle. Suddenly Jess saw a way out – she could get rid of this problem right now by *becoming* her mum. Mrs Ashton wasn't a friend of Mum's – she probably didn't even know Mum worked in the library – so if she'd never spoken to her before . . .

'Oh, hellair!' trilled Jess, diving into a Posh Mum identity. 'How awwwful for you! But dain't worry – you'll be abslooctly faine!'

Granny paused in her loading of the dishwasher and stared across the kitchen in surprise.

'What happens, though?' asked Mrs Ashton

inconveniently. It seemed she was determined to have the whole hysterectomy described in gory detail.

'Fffrankly, I can't remember much abight it!' Jess went on, turning up the poshness from genteel to almost royal. 'They filled me with such sooper anaesthetic, I don't remember a thing! The nurses were sweethearts! When I came round I felt a bit woozy for a few minutes, but from then on it was flowers and choccies for weeks on end!'

Granny approached Jess, her face transfixed with curiosity. Jess turned her back and tried to wave her away.

'But didn't it hurt?' persisted Beatrice's mum anxiously. 'And when you came round, how many drips and things did you have?'

'Oh, just the usual ones, you know!' Jess went on. Her experience of drips was limited to taps that hadn't been properly turned off. 'I did look a bit like an octopus for a day or two, but everybody was tairribly, tairribly kaihnd!'

'How long was it before you could walk again?' Mrs Ashton must once have worked for MI5 in the interrogation department.

Jess hesitated. How long would it take to get back on your feet if you'd had your womb removed? A sympathetic pang twanged through her tummy. Jess thought that if she ever had to have a hysterectomy, she might never walk again and would have to whizz around on a glamorous four-poster bed fitted with an outboard motor.

'Beatrice said Jess told her you were playing tennis again a couple of months later,' Mrs Ashton added, with obvious suspicion.

'Oh, that silly little Jess!' cackled Jess, sounding like a tipsy duchess at a garden party. 'She has no sense of time whatsoever! I was playing tennis again . . . Well, let me see . . . Oh deah! I'm afraid I have no sense of time, either! But it was quite soon afterwards, really – I remember the doctors were very impressed.'

'What about the hospital?' persisted Mrs Ashton grimly. 'My husband's been doing some research on it and he says it's not got a very good record on infections.'

'Oh, the horsepital was quaite, quaite lovely!' gushed Jess. 'There was the most delaightful team of cleaners who nevah stopped scrubbing from morning to naight! They deserve the Nobel Prize for Hygiene! Ha, ha!'

Mrs Ashton did not laugh. Anyone facing an operation might find it hard to retain their sense of humour, of course, especially when being counselled by a shrieking idiot.

'I see,' said Mrs Ashton thoughtfully. 'Well, maybe it won't be so bad after all.'

'Of course it wain't!' Jess assured her, praying that Mrs Ashton would soon be reassured enough to ring off and never darken their phone line again.

'Would you mind if I rang again?' enquired Mrs Ashton, clearly still very jittery and determined to be a nuisance. 'If I think of any more questions?'

Oh no! Jess broke into a cold sweat. She hadn't been through this whole charade in order for Bea's mum to ring up *again*! Mrs Ashton might get through to Mum herself next time, and Mum would obviously be puzzled to discover that she had inadvertently experienced major surgery while mysteriously living as a duchess in a small terraced house in an unfashionable part of town.

'I'm so sorry!' Jess's brain went into overdrive. 'I'm orf skiing tomorrow! To Saint . . .' What was that skiing place named after a saint? Oh glory! Jess's mind, paralysed suddenly by the white-hot energy it had been pumping out in the last minute or two, went blindly and totally blank. 'Saint . . .' she stuttered. 'Oh, what's the name of the wretched place? I think it begins with an M.'

'Saint Michael?' suggested Mrs Ashton feebly.

'No, no, that's what it says on the label on my undies! Ha, ha!' brayed Jess, going half-mad in her new rampant toff identity. 'Saint . . . Saint Mirren . . . No, I think that's a football team . . . ?'

'Saint . . . Matthew?' enquired Bea's mum.

'No, no, Saint . . . errrrr . . .' Jess was convinced she was having a mental breakdown. She could feel her brain melting.

'Saint . . . Maximilian?' suggested Mrs Ashton rather startlingly.

'Goodness!' exclaimed Jess. 'You're certainly an expert when it comes to saints, aren't you?'

'Well,' Bea's mum admitted, 'I am a Catholic.'

'Ah!' Jess exclaimed. 'How lairvely!' She wasn't sure if this was the appropriate response, but at least it was complimentary.

'Saint Moritz!' Mrs Ashton blurted out. 'That's the ski place, isn't it? Is that where you're going?'

'That's it!' Jess pounced. 'You're so clever! I'm orf there tomorrow for a fortnight, so I'm afraid I won't be arind to answer any more questions! But I'm sure you'll do *brrrrilliantly*!'

'What's Saint Moritz like?' asked Mrs Ashton. 'And what's skiing like? I've never been.'

Jess's sympathy for Bea's mum began to evaporate swiftly. Instead of hoping that her op would go well, Jess was now praying that the surgeon, in a moment of absent-mindedness, would remove the dear lady's tongue.

'Can't tell you, I'm afraid!' Jess shrilled. 'Never been myself! It's my fairst taime! I expect I'll break a leg!'

'Oh, I do hope not!' said Mrs Ashton anxiously. 'Do let me know via Jess that you're all right. I shall think of you whizzing down the slopes!'

'And I shall think of you!' Jess assured her. 'Whizzing down the, er, sparkling clean horsepital corridors on your lairvely trolley! Hope it goes well! Fingers crossed! Do let me know via Beatrice how you're doing!'

'Well, goodbye, then,' said Mrs Ashton, managing to make it sound ominous, even terminal. 'And thanks so much for talking to me.'

'It's been an absloot pleasure!' cried Jess. 'Toodle-pip!'

She replaced the phone with an exhausted groan of torment, and slowly turned around to discover, standing and staring at her, not only Granny, but also Mum, who was swathed in bath towels and boggling for England.

'What on earth was all that about?' Mum demanded, looking rather ratty. 'Who were you talking to?' Of course, she was bound to be grumpy for a few days now Martin had abandoned her.

'I was just rehearsing a comedy sketch with Fred,' said Jess, quickly reaching for the only excuse she could think of.

Strangely, Mum's brow cleared and a smile of relief lit up her face. 'Oh, so you're back together again?' she exclaimed. 'How lovely! We were just saying earlier how much we all like Fred and how we were hoping you'd patch it up soon. Dad wants to invite him round for supper – I think he's planning something special with sea bass. When can Fred come? Tomorrow?'

Chapter 9

'No!' gasped Jess, feeling giddy as yet another crisis seemed to engulf her. 'Don't invite him round! We're not *that* together! We're only working on a few sketches, that's all.'

'Ah, well, that's a lovely start, isn't it, dear?' said Granny with a naughty twinkling smile. 'I'm sure one thing will soon lead to another . . .'

'No, Granny!' shouted Jess.

She absolutely had to get this understood right now. She was still reeling from that stupid phone call with Mrs Ashton – all that had happened just because she'd told Beatrice what she wanted to hear, had tried to reassure her that her mum's op was going to be OK and that she would get better, and fast. She'd only been trying to be nice and supportive for goodness' sake, but for some reason she'd been punished for it, big time.

Suddenly the phone rang – again. Jess dived for it. It had to be Mrs Ashton again! What now? More punishment for being nice?

'Hello?' she said, trying to sound posh enough to be the faux Madeleine Jordan, but not too posh to be herself if that was what was required.

'Hello, sweetheart!' It was Dad. 'Guess what! I've got a job!'

'Congratulations, Dad!' Jess almost yelped with relief and joy. 'Where?'

'Oh, it's nothing special,' he went on, almost gabbling in his excitement, bless him. 'I'll tell you all about it when I get home. See you soon! Bye!'

'Dad's got a job,' she reported.

Mum's face brightened. 'Oh, good!' she beamed. 'Then maybe he'll be able to find a place of his own and you can have your room back. I'm sorry it's been a bit tricky for you, Jess.'

'Oh, it's OK,' said Jess with a saintly shrug. She might as well burrow deep into Mum's good books while she had the chance because any minute now Mrs Ashton might ring again for some more pre-op counselling.

Mum went back upstairs to get dressed, and Granny toddled off to catch the news bulletin just in case there were any juicy new murders. Jess loitered guiltily in the kitchen and then moved the phone slightly off its cradle so nobody would be able to call.

As she strolled off to join Granny in her den, an annoying thought crossed Jess's mind. OK, Mrs Ashton wouldn't be able to get through, but neither would Fred. The annoying thing about this thought wasn't that Fred wouldn't be able to ring her, but that she'd had the thought in the first place. Fred was supposed to be wiped right off her memory banks.

'I am so over him!' she told herself sternly. 'I have to forget him now. He let me down really, really badly and even if he did ring, I wouldn't want to speak to him, would I?'

When Dad arrived he brought fish and chips with him straight from the chippy.

'Congrats, Dad!' Jess gave him a big hug. 'What's this job, then?'

'Oh, nothing exciting,' said Dad. 'I'm going to be a postman. I'm quite looking forward to it actually – delivering birthday cards and keeping an eye on various old dears, you know.'

'Yes, you always were good with old people,' remarked Mum, putting the fish and chips into the oven to heat them up a bit. 'You always get on well with Granny, don't you?'

'I'm not old!' protested Granny. 'I'm just very thoroughly middle-aged.'

'Well, I see it as my mission to look after the people on my round,' said Dad. 'Cheer them up, you know.'

'You can start by cheering Madeleine up,' said Granny, laying the table and glancing anxiously at Mum. 'Martin's staying in Canada.'

'What?' Dad looked shocked. 'Why?'

'He's back with his ex,' said Granny bitterly. 'I always had a feeling he wasn't very reliable.'

'Oh dear.' Dad looked crushed. 'I didn't have that feeling at all. I thought he was great and you two seemed very well suited. You deserve somebody nice.' He looked at Mum with a serious, rather loyal expression, a bit like a sad spaniel.

'Oh, do let's stop all this gloomy talk!' snapped Mum. 'Martin and I were just ships that passed in the night, that's all.'

'It is odd, though,' mused Granny. 'First Tim gets the old heave-ho from Phil, then Jess and Fred have a bust-up and now this.' She looked a bit *too* interested in the disintegration of her family's relationships – as if she was hoping it might result in a homicide.

'Well, thanks for drawing attention to the fact that we're all basically unlovable,' said Mum. It was supposed to be a joke, but it didn't sound much like one.

'I'm not unlovable!' protested Jess. 'I dumped Fred, not vice versa!' She was aware, however, that mysteriously it didn't really feel like that.

'Anyway, Granny,' said Dad with a playful grin, 'cheer up! You're the only one who hasn't been dumped.'

'You wait till your loved one dies,' observed Granny grimly. 'Then you'll feel dumped, believe me.'

'Oh dear, I'm so sorry!' Dad exclaimed. 'Me and my big mouth! Let me get you a drink! I've bought a bottle of wine!'

'I won't have wine, thank you, Tim,' said Granny sniffily. 'I'll just have a cup of tea after my supper, as usual.'

Jess felt a bit sorry for Dad. He'd come home in high spirits, wanting to celebrate and be proud of his new job, and everybody was being a bit stressy and negative.

'Well, I'll have a mug of hot chocolate, Dad!' She beamed and hugged him again. 'I want to celebrate your new job! Can I come and help you with all the old ladies?'

'I'm not sure,' said Dad warily. 'Give me a bit of time to get settled in and then I'll let you know. I expect some of them will be real characters.'

'What's the money like?' asked Mum, still a bit grumpy because of her recent heartbreak. 'Peanuts, I expect.'

Jess felt cross with her for dissing Dad's job already.

'Worse than peanuts,' grinned Dad. 'But never mind – it'll be enough to get a room somewhere, so soon I'll be out of your hair.'

It was odd, thinking of Dad living in a bedsit as if he was a student or something. As they ate the fish and chips, Jess contrasted her dad's life story so far with Flora's father's. Mr Barclay had built up a successful business, but suddenly, out of the blue, and because of something happening with banks in the USA and Europe – she'd never quite understood it – his business was tottering on the edge of a precipice and he wasn't much better off than Dad. Maybe Flora's dad would leave Flora's mum and he and Jess's dad could share a flat! Jess smiled to herself at the thought of the dads trying to get on. It would be the perfect sitcom, if only Fred was available as a comedy-writing partner.

Oh no! She'd thought about Fred again! Jess was quite cross with herself. She mustn't think about him again this evening, even though there was English homework and they had often collaborated on it via Skype.

This helped to deal with the basic awfulness of having to do homework, as Fred often appeared on Skype wearing fancy dress, or at least a range of silly hats which he had conjured up from old cornflake packets and bunches of bananas. No! She absolutely mustn't think of Fred!

Although Dad was staying in her room these days, Jess still used her desk for homework, so after supper she picked up her school bag and trailed listlessly upstairs. She fought off a desire to see Fred wearing a silly hat – the last one had been rabbit ears. No, no! She mustn't think of Fred *at all*. As she reached the top of the stairs, she consciously suppressed all images of Fred wearing comedy headgear, then she stepped inside her bedroom.

Her desk was on the right, up against the wall, and above it was a pinboard, totally plastered with photos of herself and Fred. There were photos they'd taken in the park last summer, with Fred lying under a tree covered with sheets of paper all scribbled out – the comedy sketch they'd been working on. There were photos of Fred in St Ives when they'd gone to see Dad. Fred on Porthmeor Beach with an enormous sand-mouse (they'd decided sandcastles were too much of a cliché). There was a photo of Fred looking straight into the camera very tenderly, but with a clothes peg on his nose.

Slowly, miserably, Jess started unpinning the photos from the board and placing them in the top drawer of her desk. All the various Freds accumulated there in a pile, some of the lower Freds peeping out around the edges. The pinboard now looked bare and sad. Jess closed the drawer.

But now, of course, she had to open the drawer again to get her pen out, and there were the Freds again, looking at her, frozen in various happy times in the past. Irritated, Jess went into her mum's study and found a large padded envelope. She put all the Freds in there and then placed the envelope in the bottom of her wardrobe. Her whole room was strangely tidy these days, now Dad was staying there, So the envelope looked very obvious and somehow tragic. If only there was the usual heap of garbage on her floor! Then she could have hidden the Freds under six grubby sweaters.

Jess sighed and went back to her desk. She closed her eyes and took a deep breath. Then she switched on her laptop. Instantly she saw that George had Facebooked her. George was the older brother of Jack Stevens, Flora's boyfriend, and he'd been at the Chaos

Dinner Dance which had caused all this trouble between Jess and Fred.

Hey, Jess! his message went. *We took a video of your hosting routine with Fred and we've posted it on YouTube.* He gave a URL in case she wanted to take a look.

Oh no! At the very moment she was trying so hard to obliterate Fred from her consciousness, that awful hosting routine which he'd hijacked had been preserved for posterity and posted on the freaking internet! Now the last ghastly moments of their relationship could be seen and ridiculed by everybody in the whole wide world!

Chapter 10

'Right,' said Mr Fothergill next morning after registration. 'I think this latest craze for Scrabble is to be encouraged. So I've bought a copy of *The Scrabble Dictionary* to settle any disputes, and we're going to have a Scrabble competition. The prize is fifty pounds' worth of gift tokens, kindly donated by an anonymous well-wisher. It's obviously going to be more fun if you work in teams, so I want you all paired up by lunch-time so we can set it up properly.'

Flora grabbed Jess's arm. 'You're my partner!' she whispered urgently. 'We're gonna win that fifty pounds, babe – you and me are the A-team.'

'Yeah,' replied Jess. 'You bet!'

But deep down she felt a sickening stab of regret. If she and Fred hadn't broken up, they would so obviously have been the A-team – not that Flora wasn't one of the cleverest people in the class, with straight As for every subject under the sun, but somehow the whole Scrabble competition would have been such a glorious opportunity for her and Fred to have a laugh together, and now . . .

Fred was sitting at the front of the class, over by the window, and somehow he blotted out everything else, even though Jess wasn't actually looking at him. She was staring instead at the back of Mackenzie's head and the way his dark curls tumbled down over his collar, and counting the thirty-seven tiny specks of dandruff on his shoulders, and listening with a fixed, false smile to Flora rabbiting on about just how brilliant their Scrabble performances were going to be.

But all Jess could see and hear was something happening way out of the shot, and almost in slow motion: Jodie, who was sitting behind Fred, reached forward and thumped him on the back, and he turned round with an outraged glare – or was it a mock outraged glare?

'Fred, you've gotta be my partner!' bawled Jodie. 'Cos you're way too brilliant, it's not fair – you've got to have a dumb partner. And let's face it, I'm the dumbest on the planet!'

'Oh no!' groaned Fred. 'I'd rather have all my teeth

pulled out, without anaesthetic, than be shackled to a moron like you for a split second!'

'I'll take that as a yes!' yelled Jodie in triumph, punching the air. And Jess knew all too well that it was indeed one of Fred's yeses: in fact, he'd said something similar to her once, ages ago, when they'd first started going out together. It had sounded like a put-down, but it had been, back then, the closest thing to a declaration of love that Fred was ever likely to produce.

Then, still in slow motion, Fred turned back, away from Jodie, and for a split second his eyes met Jess's (her gaze had somehow wandered from the fascinating sight of Mackenzie's dandruff). As their eyes locked, for a moment Jess felt a stab of pain in her innermost secret heart, but she did her best to disguise it with a bold, indifferent stare. Fred's eyes were strange – shifty, almost, mysterious, not giving anything away – and all too soon they slithered off elsewhere, and it was as if the moment had never been.

On the way to history, Jess tuned back into Flora's monologue. She seemed to be talking about the trials of moving her stuff out of her bedroom and into Freya's room.

'Freya's wardrobe is full of clothes she hasn't worn

for years. I mean, she hasn't even bothered to take them to uni with her, but because of that, there's hardly any room for mine, it's so tight!' she wailed. 'And when she comes home at Easter and I have to share with Felicity, we're going to have to fit twin beds into her room and her room's the smallest – it's so not fair! There's barely enough room for her and me to have a bed each. Both our beds will have to be up against a wall!'

'Welcome to the real world,' said Jess sarcastically. 'My bed has been up against a wall for years. In fact, it's so far up against the wall, it's practically on the ceiling.'

'Oh!' Flora gasped. 'I didn't mean – but your bedroom is lovely, Jess. It couldn't be nicer, it's so cosy.' *Cosy* meant *small*, of course.

'Yeah, right,' said Jess, trying not to sound too stressy. She was still a bit cross with Flora, though, for being so tactless. Flo knew perfectly well that Jess and her mum had always been hard up and always lived in a small terraced house. For Flora to present her current crisis as a tragedy was, well, just insensitive.

'I'm sorry, babe,' whispered Flora, taking Jess's arm. 'I'm saying stupid things and getting it all wrong. I just feel so mixed up about everything.' Two tiny pearly tears slid down her cheeks.

Oh no! Now Jess had to cheer *her* up! Jess felt deeply sorry for poor Flo, but also somehow irritated that she'd turned on the waterworks, because if somebody's in tears it somehow moves the goalposts. If you were in the right and they were in the wrong, that doesn't matter any more once those darned little drops of water are rolling down their cheeks.

Jess gave her a hug. 'Cheer up, you legend!' she murmured. 'Wipe away those tears! No, wait! Cry some more!' *Comedy might help*, thought Jess. 'We could bottle them and sell 'em to your admirers in Year Seven. They could be the answer to the cash flow problem. Tell your dad you've got a business plan – if you cry all day five days a week, you could probably be a millionaire by the middle of next year.'

Flora laughed and wiped her eyes, and they arrived for history. As they entered, somebody barged into them. It was Fred.

'I've forgotten my . . .' he hesitated, looking panicky.

'Brain?' enquired Jess sweetly.

'No, no,' Fred muttered, his eyes kind of roaming around the world in search of something. 'I've forgotten my . . . role in life. I must've left it in my locker. Excuse me.' And he pushed past them and ran off down the corridor.

They exchanged puzzled looks. Flora arched a perfectly plucked eyebrow.

'What was that all about?' she wondered.

'Oh, he's just forgotten his history book,' said Jess, and she looked around the classroom for a place to sit.

Where had Fred been installed? Jess's eyes raced across the room. She had to sit as far away as possible from him. With a sickening lurch she saw it: right at the back, and wearing a very complacent smirk, Jodie was sitting next to an empty chair which had Fred's anorak hanging over the back of it. Jodie's arm was stretched along the back of Fred's chair, almost cuddling the anorak as if she owned it. On the empty desk was Fred's pencil case, adorned with a strip cartoon design. It was something Jess had bought for his birthday a few months ago. But now Jodie was fiddling with it. The pencil case seemed to call out to Jess silently across the room, like a baby who'd been taken away for adoption.

There were a few empty chairs at the front, as usual, so Jess gloomily sat down there. She was glad she wouldn't be able to see what was going on at the back. From now on, she realised, she had to turn her back on Fred literally as well as metaphorically.

But what had he meant by 'I've forgotten my role in

life'? Was that anything to do with her? Was it a coded message? Was it a secret sign? Did it mean that, without her, his life was hollow and meaningless? Or was it just one of Fred's random gags? Jess felt so stressed out, she was almost relieved when Mrs Arthur came in and started talking about the French Revolution.

Chapter 11

At lunchtime Jess found she wasn't very hungry. Sitting in the canteen and watching Henry Field and Ben O'Sullivan gorging on burger and chips was a disgusting enough sight, but down at the other end of the room Fred's back was clearly visible, sandwiched between Jodie and Mackenzie.

At the sight of that sandwich, Jess lost interest in her own, even though it was her absolute favourite: cheese and tomato. She took one bite, but it was like trying to eat a pair of gloves containing a dead mouse. She wrapped it in a paper napkin and stuffed it in her school bag, between her history textbook and her pencil case. She would eat it later when Fred was safely out of vision. (The sandwich, not the pencil case.)

Ben Jones drifted up, carrying a vast plate of salad. As captain of the football team he had to be a bit of a role model when it came to lunch, so his meal choices were always impeccably healthy.

'Can I, uh, join you, ladies?' he asked.

A few girls sitting nearby darted glances at him.

'Oh yes, Ben, please – we're honoured!' said Flora.

Ben carefully placed his plate of salad down opposite them. His hair was as madly blond as ever, and the dazzling Caribbean blue of his eyes was even more striking at this gloomy time of year. Looking at Ben Jones was the nearest that Jess was going to get to a tropical beach holiday, and yet she still couldn't help taking a quick peep through the crowds of people behind him, down to where Fred's back was so interestingly displayed. Oh, pants! She must stop this guilty glancing! What was so special about Fred's back, anyway? It was, if anything, one of his worst features – thin, knobbly and slightly round-shouldered.

'Ben, are you growing your hair?' asked Flora. 'It looks kind of longer or something.'

'Uh, yeah. No – maybe. I haven't really thought about it,' murmured BJ. 'Maybe I just forgot about it for a while.' He turned his wonderful blue eyes to Jess. 'I saw your, er, hosting routine thing on YouTube,' he said. 'Hilarious!' He smiled.

A year ago, Jess's heart would have melted into a tiny pool of twinkling champagne at this point, but things had changed so much that now she found it almost impossible to concentrate on what beautiful Ben was saying as long as Fred's bony but charismatic back was clearly visible through the throng.

'I wish George hadn't put that routine up on YouTube,' sighed Jess. 'It was one of the worst evenings of my life and I really don't want to be reminded of it.'

Ben's smiled faded and his wonderful eyes darkened sympathetically into saintly concern. 'Why?' he asked. 'It was a – you know, a triumph.'

'It was Fred's triumph.' Jess pushed her plate away. She felt guilty at being so stressy about the whole thing. Ben, though no longer her crush, had become one of her dearest friends. He always seemed concerned and supportive. However, being in another class, he wasn't quite up to speed on the details of her break-up with Fred.

'Mackenzie said . . .' Ben frowned at his salad and began to toy with it with his fork. 'You and Fred, uh . . .'

'We're history,' said Jess, trying to make it sound quite comfortable and over – done and dusted.

'Oh no! I'm sorry!' Ben put his fork down again. He hadn't even tasted his coleslaw yet. 'I thought it might be just a . . . a blip. Is that the right word? What is a blip, exactly?'

'It's just a temporary thing,' explained Flora, sensing that help would be welcome, conversation-wise. 'From, you know – electronics, I think. A temporary loss of power or something.'

'I'm such a dumbo when it comes to words.' Ben smiled sadly at his salad mountain. 'Did you hear there's going to be this Scrabble competition? My worst nightmare, sort of . . .' For a minute it seemed as if he was going to say something else, but in the end he just sighed and plunged his fork into a portion of tomato salad.

'I'm such a dumbo when it comes to words, too!' Flora assured him. Ben gave her a sceptical look. Everyone knew Flora was top of the class in almost everything. 'But luckily,' she went on, 'Jess has agreed to be my partner, and with her wit and genius, we're gonna sweep the competition right off the map.'

'Anyway,' Jess added, 'you don't need words when you can play football the way you do. And how much do top footballers make per week? A bit more than Scrabble aces, I believe!' She beamed at him. Curiously, for one so glamorously fit, Ben had confidence issues.

'Well . . .' Ben hesitated, chewing a few leaves of rocket. 'Money's not everything.'

Jess knew she'd made a mistake by mentioning the slightly tricky subject of money because Flora might be a bit sensitive about not having any nowadays. Before she could say anything to change the subject, though, down at the far end of the canteen, Fred suddenly got up – a startling moment, and one which inexplicably caused her heart to leap and thump. At the same time as enduring these symptoms, Jess silently reproached herself for her foolishness. Fred had got up into a standing position! Oh my! If only the BBC and CNN had been here to record the momentous occasion!

He was now carrying his tray to stack it on the trolley. Even though he was right down at the other end of the room, Jess could see that he hadn't left any of his lunch. His appetite was evidently completely unaffected by their break-up, then – unlike hers. So maybe as far as he was concerned, everything really was hunky-dory, done and dusted, history.

Now he turned to face in her direction. Jess switched her gaze back towards Ben. Oh no! Ben was saying something and she hadn't been listening! Even now she couldn't concentrate, because Fred had to walk right past them to leave the canteen.

Would he look at her? How would she ever know if he was going to look at her, though? Because, whatever happened, she mustn't look at him. What would happen if their eyes met? Would his gaze be cold and distant, or would there be a little electric shock of something or other – a sign that maybe things weren't quite as done and dusted as all that, and not quite history, in other words? And was that the way she wanted things to be?

She focused desperately on Ben's lips, which were still moving, and his eyes, which were fixed on her.

'You don't, uh, have to come if you don't want to,' he concluded.

'Of course I'll come!' beamed Jess recklessly. Come where? What was this thing she'd just committed to? Would it involve physical pain? Before anything could be made clear, Jess's mind went whirling off into free fall again because she could see that Fred, Mackenzie and Jodie weren't just heading for the door – they were approaching this very table. Jodie arrived first – of course.

'Hey, you lot!' she shrieked. 'We challenge you to a Scrabble game right now, back at the Art Room! Not part of the tournament thing, just a practice, a warm-up, a friendly.'

'Or an unfriendly, if you prefer,' added Fred, cocking his left eyebrow quizzically and glancing lightly in her direction. What did he mean by *that*?

'I'm their trainer,' said Mackenzie. 'I flap towels at them between rounds and give them pep talks!'

'Shall we?' Flora asked, giving Jess a very understanding look. Did Jess want a Scrabble game with her ex? Was it such a good idea?

'Yeah, why not?' Jess stared boldly at Fred. 'You'll have to break the habit of a lifetime, though.'

'What's that?' asked Fred. 'Not let you win for a change?'

'No!' snapped Jess, but trying to make it quite a light-hearted snap. 'No cheating!'

'My dear lady, when have I ever cheated?' asked Fred.

There was a brief, awkward pause, as Jess couldn't think of anything to say. She could feel herself getting hot. Cheating had a double meaning. OK, Fred hadn't cheated on her, but how long would it be before he did? But wait. He wasn't her boyfriend now. She shouldn't be thinking like this.

'Come on, then, let's get on with it.' Flora rescued the conversation and got to her feet.

Jess followed. 'Excuse us, Ben,' she apologised. Ben

had only just started his lunch, after all, and now they were leaving.

He waved away her apology and smiled. 'No worries, good luck,' he said. 'See you later.'

As they walked off, Jess wondered when exactly she would see Ben next because she knew she'd committed herself to something. But, first and foremost, how on earth was she going to cope with playing Scrabble with Fred and Jodie?

Chapter 12

'Right!' Jodie grabbed a Scrabble board and slapped it down on the table. 'Are you ready, partner?' she said, grinning across at Fred. She pronounced 'partner' like people do in Westerns: 'podner'. 'We're gonna whup you outta sight!' she informed Jess and Flora.

'I wonder if the term "whup" is in *The Scrabble Dictionary*?' asked Jess in a posh headmistressy voice. 'I think you'll find most of Jodie's vocab is mysteriously absent.'

'Mysteriously absent,' repeated Fred, rubbing his hands together thoughtfully. 'Interesting phrase. Good name for a band, or possibly a dog. I might adopt it as my motto. Mysteriously absent . . . hmmm.'

Jess's heart gave a tiny skip. Did Fred mean what she thought he meant? But then, what did she think he meant? After all, she was mysteriously absent from his life. Except that she was sitting right next to him. She sighed and plunged her hand into the Scrabble bag, pulling out a P.

'Did you want to have a P?' enquired Fred. Jodie laughed coarsely. Fred pulled a U out.

'I'd rather have P than U,' retorted Jess, and shot him a sidelong glance. He wasn't looking her way, though. It was so awkward, him not being her partner. If he had been, he'd be sitting opposite her now and eye contact would be effortless. Now, if she wanted to engage in eye contact with Fred, she practically had to dislocate her neck. He was sitting opposite Jodie, of course, and for all Jess knew, when he looked across at Jodie his eyes might wander from her face towards what had recently become Jodie's prize assets – boobs the size of airbags.

Despite frequent prayers, exercises recommended by a website and a secret cream which had given her an itchy rash, Jess's own bosom remained tastefully bijou. She wondered just how important breasts really were. Obviously, in the natural course of things, having small breasts didn't matter, and she'd always apologised to God when starting one of her regular prayers requesting divine breast augmentation. However, she was aware that certain celebrities had built whole careers on nothing else but a massive superstructure, and she had to admit that Jodie's bust was one of the wonders of the modern world.

Flora fished out an A. (Of course! Straight As in everything, even Scrabble games.) This meant she had to start, and had first pick of the letters. After Flora had picked hers out of the bag, it was Fred's turn, and as he passed the bag to Jess, their fingers touched fleetingly. Fred showed no sign of being aware of it. But was he? Had he secretly been thrilled at the brief moment of skin contact? Was his heart also racing slightly faster than usual? If not, why was hers? Jess was annoyed with her body. It seemed kind of needy, and that was the very opposite of how she wanted to appear.

Jess pulled out seven letters: E, E, E, I, O, S and X. She was pleased about the X, which was a valuable letter, but the terrible plague of Es irritated her. There were only a couple of really embarrassing possibilities: SEX and EX, neither of which could be used; SEX for obvious reasons and EX because her very own ex was sitting right next to her.

'Oh dear, this is so rubbish,' complained Flora, moving her letters about.

'And with that, she put down ANGSTY on a double word score,' drawled Fred.

'Is ANGSTY in the book?' demanded Jodie.

'It's not angsty,' Flora announced, placing INSANE on the board.

'Waste of an S,' commented Fred, counting up Flora's score and writing it down.

'Why?' asked Flora, her eyes wide and puzzled.

'You should always save your S,' said Fred, fiddling with his own letters. 'Then you can put it at the end of somebody's word and get double points for changing their word to a new one.'

'What? What?' Flora shook her head in bewilderment. 'I've hardly ever played Scrabble before.'

'Suppose somebody had put DOG down,' Fred explained. 'You could add an S to the end of DOG, making DOGS, and your S could be part of a different word, say, something like SECRET. So you'd have double the score.'

'Oh no!' cried Flora. 'Is it too late? Can I take my S back?'

'No, you can't!' snapped Fred with a sadistic grin. 'It's my turn now!'

'Tight!' Flora pouted.

Fred ignored her, and with a flourish, placed the word QUEST on the board.

'Brilliant score, partner!' yelled Jodie, punching the

air. 'A, Q and a U! The gods of Scrabble are certainly smiling on us!'

'But you just told me I'd wasted my S!' wailed Flora. 'And now you've done the exact same thing!'

'I think you'll find we already have an unassailable lead,' said Fred, turning to Jess with a smirk. 'Do your best, Jordan, although of course we all know that won't amount to much.'

It was supposed to be a slight, bubbly kind of banter, only mock aggressive, but because of recent unpleasant events, and Jess's bruised self-esteem, what he said really hurt.

'I can't do much at all,' Jess confessed, trying to ignore her wounded heart. 'I've got more Es than a chocolate bar.'

'QUEST is such a lovely word,' said Flora suddenly. 'Don't you think? Wasn't it romantic in the good old days when guys would perform brave quests to win the hearts of their lady loves?'

Jess shot Flora a warning glance. She didn't want Flo to start on this topic.

'Luckily that's not necessary these days,' said Fred. 'As everybody knows, I'm a legendary coward. I wouldn't have lasted five minutes in medieval England.'

'Yes, you would!' Jodie beamed at him. 'You would have been the court jester.'

'No!' countered Flora. 'Jess would have been the jester. Jess the Jester – it has a certain ring to it.'

Jess was still struggling to come up with a word, preferably not involving SEX. Eventually she sighed and added an O and an E to the final T of QUEST, making TOE.

'Bravo!' cried Fred sarcastically. 'I see you've put your toe down, but it's not going to win you many points – in Formula One or this game.'

'I'll put my toe in the seat of your pants if you don't shut up,' said Jess, annoyed that she couldn't think of anything more sparkling to say.

'Shush!' cried Jodie. 'I'm trying to think! I'm so useless!' One of the nice things about Jodie was that she was prepared to make fun of herself as well as make fun of other people.

While she was thinking, Ben Jones came into the Art Room and strolled up to the Scrabble game. He leaned against the wall and studied the board. Then he went round and stood behind Jodie.

'Hard luck,' he commented sympathetically. 'I don't think, um, Polish words are allowed.' This was quite witty by Ben Jones's standards.

'Shut up!' snapped Jodie. Then she turned to Fred. 'Can I have MANK?'

'Uh, sorry to disturb the game and stuff,' said Ben, suddenly fixing his gaze on Jess in a disconcerting way, 'but I just wanted to say there's a bus that leaves Station Road at about ten to seven tonight and that gets there in time.'

Jess looked at him, her mind a total blank. What on earth was she supposed to be doing tonight? Suddenly everybody's eyes were on her. Jess felt her face fill up with red fire. What could she possibly say?

95

Chapter 13

'What's this? What's this? A date?' shrieked Jodie, a wicked grin playing on her lips.

The word 'date' was a jolt to Jess's delicate nervous system.

'Jess is coming to see the James Bond movie with us at the multiplex,' said Ben.

'Who's "us"? Is this a private party or can anybody join in?' asked Jodie.

'I thought you'd already seen it.' Fred turned to Jess and raised his sarcastic eyebrow (the left one) in a mocking way. 'I thought you saw it when you went with your mum on her blind date?'

Jess's blush deepened. Not only did it appear as if she'd suddenly rushed into dating Ben Jones, but it looked as if she was so desperate to go out with him that she'd pretended she hadn't already seen the film.

Worst of all, she was going to have to sit through two more hours of the kind of movie that made her feel violently sick. When she saw it before she'd spent much of the time with her eyes closed. But she had to hide her panic.

'It was such a great movie – I can't wait to see it again!' she lied.

Fred stared at her in disbelief. He was addicted to violent TV and films, and he'd often teased her about her squeamishness. 'But I thought madam was inclined to feel faint even when the heroines get their feet wet in Jane Austen?' enquired Fred in the same barbed tone.

'It's true, I used to hate violence,' said Jess boldly, staring at him as violently as possible – so violently that her eyeballs actually twanged. 'But I've had a change of heart. I love violence now – only on screen at the moment, but as time goes by I might end up dishing it out.'

'Oh no! I must get myself a bodyguard!' exclaimed Fred.

'Anyway,' interrupted Jodie, 'can we come or is it a date?'

Ben shifted his feet about in an embarrassed way and the faintest hint of a blush spread over his cheeks. 'No, no, it's a . . . a gang of us going,' he said awkwardly.

Jess's heart gave a kind of squeeze of sympathy for him. She and Ben had tried dating once or twice in the past, and it had never worked. She had realised that if you have a crush on somebody, then get over it and later try dating them, the romance somehow never works properly.

'Who else is coming?' demanded Jodie. Ben hesitated and blushed some more. Jess had a sudden horrible feeling that Ben hadn't actually asked anyone else and that he was too embarrassed to think of anybody else who might possibly come.

'My cousin,' he said. 'You know, Melissa – she helped with Chaos.'

'Oh, the girl doing the cloakroom thing?' exclaimed Jodie. 'She's amazing. She looks a bit kind of Russian, don't you think, Jess?'

'Not really,' said Jess grumpily.

'Anyway, can we come?' asked Jodie.

Ben appeared to flinch slightly. 'Sure,' he said, with a faint unconvincing smile.

'I can't come.' Flora shook her head. 'I have to sort my stuff out tonight and decide what I'm going to sell on eBay. Jack's coming over to help.' Jack was in the Sixth Form so he and Flora never really got to hang out together in school – only Sixth Formers were allowed in the Common Room and Jack wouldn't be seen dead anywhere else, so their relationship depended heavily on out-of-school contact.

'Well, I can come and so can Fred, can't you, Fred?' Jodie barged on in her domineering way.

Fred shrugged limply. 'I was planning a lovely evening staring at my bedroom wall,' he said. 'But I suppose duty comes before pleasure.'

'Eh?' gasped Jodie, puzzled. Jess sighed inwardly. How could Fred bear to spend time with a girl who hardly understood a word he said?

'I *will* go to the ball!' Fred confirmed, looking up at Ben.

'OK, brilliant,' said Ben. 'See you all at ten to seven, then, at the Station Road bus stop.'

'Except me,' added Flora. 'I hope you guys have fun.'

Precisely six hours later the fun began. Jess arrived at the bus stop to find Ben, Fred and Jodie already there. Jodie was wearing a stripy top and high heels and looked disastrously attractive. Jess herself had dressed down in leggings and some layers. The agony about what to wear had been even worse than usual because she didn't want to look as if she'd made an effort to look glam for Ben, but on the other hand, she didn't want Fred to think she looked frumpy. Luckily it was winter! She took refuge in her parka and a rather divine pink fluffy scarf which had been knitted for her by her Dad's ex-boyfriend Phil.

'Hi, Jess!' yelled Jodie. 'Guess what! Melissa's not coming! Nor are any of her friends! They've all got "food poisoning"!' Jodie raised both her hands and gave the speech marks sign in the air to indicate that Ben's pathetic excuse revealed the truth – that he and Jess had been on a date, or at least had been planning to go to a movie alone together, which amounted to the same thing. And as they were now a 'foursome' (*speech marks in the air again*, thought Jess), did that make this evening a double date?

Jodie got on the bus first and Jess followed – Ben was standing back politely and Fred was in some kind of tangle with his pockets, looking for his wallet. Jodie went down the bus and bagged a window seat – Jodie always *bagged* a seat; she never just sat down. Jess plonked herself down beside her. Jodie turned and gave her an indignant look. She'd evidently been saving the seat for Fred but Jess was equally deter-mined to make the evening as little like a date as possible.

'So, Jodie,' she said calmly. 'How are things?'

Jodie looked startled at this sudden conversational politeness. 'Oh no!' she exclaimed, ignoring the opportunity for polite conversation. 'The guys have gone upstairs!' The seats around them were all occupied.

'I expect they'll be talking about football or something,' said Jess.

Jodie looked exasperated and bad-tempered, then her face cleared. 'Jess,' she said, suddenly sounding genuine and dropping her voice from its normal deafening volume to something barely audible, 'I hope you don't mind me and Fred being Scrabble partners, do you? I know if you hadn't broken up you'd have been his partner probably, but after all, things are different now, aren't they? *Do* you mind?' Her face looked a bit anxious and vulnerable, and Jess felt a pang of affection for her, which was inconvenient as she'd been cultivating a nice toasty hatred of Jodie as Fred's chief stalker and the president of his fan club.

'Oh no, don't worry about *that*,' she said airily, making it sound totally unimportant. 'Fred can do anything he likes. I don't own him. I never did.'

'And do you mind us coming along to see this movie?' Jodie whispered. 'Ben wanted it to be just you and him, didn't he?'

'Ben and I don't do dating,' Jess informed her loftily. 'We tried once before and it didn't work. We're just buddies.'

Jodie looked relieved. She wasn't a bad person, really, and it wasn't her fault she was growing bigger in what are sometimes called *the right places*. Jess endured a wave of sympathy for Jodie, but reserved the right, if Jodie ever did manage to sweep Fred off his feet, to hate her with renewed venom and possibly plan a terrible revenge involving a very hot curry and some tennis rackets.

The movie was difficult for several reasons. First, Jess was sitting at the end of a row, on the aisle, next to Ben. Jodie had somehow engineered this, so that she was placed between Fred and Ben and, to Jess's horror, on the far side of Fred, further along the row, was a girl of almost illegal beauty. She had long silky dark hair and lips like wet cherries. It made Jess realise that now she and Fred weren't an item any more, there wasn't just Jodie to worry about – there were literally millions of pretty girls all over the world who would be bumping into Fred at every opportunity. The particular stunner sitting next to him now appeared to be accompanied by a fat man with a moustache. There was no doubt in Jess's mind that by the end of the movie, Fred and the girl would be practically engaged.

The next dose of torment involved the film itself. It started with a car chase along a mountainous road with a sheer drop on one side. James Bond and the guys chasing him were driving like maniacs while shooting at one another with sub-machine guns. If there was one thing Jess hated, it was a sheer drop accompanied by men driving irresponsibly. Machine guns were also well down her list of desirable accessories. She closed her eyes and waited till the deafening sound effects modulated into a sudden silence. Then she opened her eyes, hoping for some respite, but found she was just in time to see a car in flames plunging down a canyon. She just knew she was going to have nightmares about this moment for the next six weeks.

There was a brief lull while the camera panned over the rooftops of a quaint Italian hill town (that was the bit Mum had enjoyed), but within seconds, instead of sitting in a pavement cafe and ordering a latte, like any sane person would have done, Bond got involved in a fight in a huge building filled with scaffolding. As he exchanged gunfire while swinging to and fro on ropes, crashing through glass skylights and leaping along collapsing girders, Jess couldn't help contrasting

Bond's adventures with the home life of her dad, whose happiest times had been spent painting seagulls. (Painting pictures of seagulls, that is.) Dad would probably faint if somebody showed him a photograph of a machine gun. Thank goodness there was a range of male character types available in real life and luckily not all men were testosterone-fuelled action heroes.

Eventually, after Mr Bond had survived approximately ninety-nine scenarios which would have reduced a lesser man to mincemeat, the film ended and Jess opened her eyes again.

'So . . . ?' Ben turned to her and stretched. His stretching, she had to admit, had the grace of a leopard. 'How about . . . uh, a coffee?'

'Great idea!' beamed Jess. Would the ordeal never end?

Chapter 14

There was a cafe in the multiplex, and they found a corner table and got some coffees. Jodie seemed full of energy – she was humming the movie's theme tune and tapping her cup with her teaspoon as if it was a drum kit. Jess became aware that she had a slight headache.

'Terrific movie,' Ben Jones was saying, looking shyly from Fred to Jess. 'That scene where they . . . uh, have the fight in speedboats.'

'Yeah!' cried Jodie loudly. 'And the scene where they jumped out of the plane! How did they film that?'

'It's probably all computer generated,' said Fred, trying to sound expert.

'No way is it all computer generated, you moron!' yelled Jodie.

Jess felt annoyed that Jodie had the barefaced cheek to call Fred 'moron' – that was her job. There was something presumptuous about it and it somehow underlined the fact that Fred was no longer Jess's boyfriend. Jess was sure Jodie wouldn't have called him 'moron' if he and Jess had still been together. It was almost flirtatious.

Or was it? There turned out to be many awful things about breaking up – more than she'd anticipated when she rather grandly dumped him after he hijacked her comedy routine. One of the awful things was that Fred seemed to have forgotten that they had ever been together. He didn't give her special secret looks, he seemed quite happy to make jokes for just anybody, he cheerfully accepted insults and aggressive behaviour from Jodie – in fact, he seemed to thrive on it. Jess had hoped that after being dumped, he would be so desperate to get back into her good books that he'd be sulking and weird with everybody, sending her scorching looks of torment all the time and cooking up a really spectacular act of heroism to impress her. But Fred was acting as if nothing in the world was the matter.

'If only more guys were like James Bond!' sighed Jodie. 'Imagine having somebody like that to protect you!'

'I don't know . . .' Jess hesitated. 'I'm not sure he's my type. It would be rather tiring.'

'Don't you fancy Daniel Craig, though?' asked Jodie. 'He's well fit. What an amazing torso! He even looked good when he had that nosebleed.'

'Hmmm . . .' Jess pondered. She didn't want to get drawn into a stupid lust fest with Jodie. 'How *did* they film that bit where they jumped out of the plane?' she asked, turning to Ben Jones.

'Well, they used a . . . um, vertical wind tunnel.'

'What's that?'

'It's, like, a kind of tube thing and wind comes up from the bottom and you can actually float about in it, but it's not, like, totally, uhhhh, um, closed in . . . so the bit where you're flying is, like, open and you can see the sky and stuff.'

'Amazing! I'd so love to do that!' yelled Jodie.

'They only filmed those bits thirty seconds at a time for safety reasons,' Ben went on. 'And they wore special contact lenses so they could keep their eyes open.'

'CGI has totally changed the Bond films,' said Fred enthusiastically. 'In parts of the film, they superimposed Daniel Craig's head on the torso of a stuntman.'

'Wonderful!' enthused Jess. 'Like a facelift, only a bit more cutting edge. If only somebody would super-impose Lara Croft's face on my torso.'

'They should impose Lara's torso as well,' said Fred.

Just a few days ago, this would have been a harmless tease. Now it really hurt.

'You don't need Lara's head or torso,' retorted Ben chivalrously.

There was an uneasy pause. This was dangerous territory – Jess's former crush complimenting her after she'd just been dissed by her ex.

'I wouldn't mind her name, though,' Jess said, hastily changing the subject. 'I'd love to be called Lara O'Hara. A rhyming name – so stylish!'

'Jess . . .' Jodie rolled her eyes, always looking for a joke. 'Jess . . . Mess.'

'Jess Bless,' said Ben, smiling.

'Jess Confess,' said Fred. 'Jess . . . Jess Less.' For a moment he hesitated and their eyes met. Fred was Jess-less now, of course.

'Leopardess,' said Ben.

'Jess,' added Jodie. 'Egg and Cress.'

'I sometimes don't like knowing how they do special effects. You know, when they're jumping over rooftops and you find out they had wires and harnesses and stuff, it spoils it.'

'They do still hurt themselves, though,' Jodie put in. 'I think Daniel Craig sliced the top off his finger and he had to have some stitches on his face.'

'I wonder what happened to the fingertip?' mused Fred. 'If I'd been working on the set, I'd have nicked it to sell on eBay.'

'I heard that it grew back,' said Jodie.

'Grew back!' exclaimed Fred with a smile. 'How, exactly? He's not a shark!'

'Healed, then,' said Jodie. 'He's got lovely hands, anyway.'

Jess felt a deep restlessness. Despite the fact that she liked Jodie, was very fond of Ben and, of course, had until recently madly adored Fred, being here together in this foursome seemed uneasy and odd. The conversation didn't flow, Fred's jokes seemed laboured and Jodie's grasshopper mind that jumped from subject to subject was irritating now, even though at other times it was entertaining, while Ben Jones was tapping the tabletop with his finger as if he would rather have been almost anywhere else. But they all had to sit there and pretend to be enjoying themselves until it was time to get the bus home.

Jess had been longing to get home, but Mum greeted her with a scowl like thunder. 'Homework!' she shouted, pointing at the clock. 'How many times do I have to tell you, you don't go out on weekday nights until you've done your homework!'

'There was no homework,' Jess lied lightly, racing upstairs. 'Mrs Martin was away, and history homework was just to revise for a test next week.'

'I don't believe you,' growled Mum, standing in the hall and glaring up the stairs at Jess's hastily departing back. 'And anyway, revision is as important as anything else. It's not *no homework*.'

Jess burst into her room to find her dad lying on her bed, reading a book.

'Oh, hi, darling!' was his response. 'How was the movie?'

Jess had forgotten, again, that he was monopolising her private space and had to hide her fury that he was there just at the very moment when she needed to call Flora and share the details of her dire evening.

'Fine, thanks, Dad,' she replied.

'And how was Fred?' asked Dad with a heavy, knowing emphasis.

'Fred was fine,' Jess lied deftly. 'Ben Jones was there, too, and Jodie. We had a coffee afterwards and talked about the special effects. I hate special effects. I like things to be real.'

She sat down at her desk and stared at her pinboard.

There was empty space now, where before there had been photos of Fred, full of fun, smiley, relaxed, not-a-care-in-the-world photos. Happy times in the past! The fact that the photos were stashed away in an envelope in the bottom of her wardrobe didn't make them less visible. Curiously, they didn't have to be literally seen because they could be felt. The contrast between those images of happy times and the scratchy evening she'd just had to endure could not have been more striking. Jess's eyes filled with tears, but with Dad in her face like this, she couldn't even shed a few private tears any more.

'I think I'll have a bath,' she said, and fled to the sanctuary of the bathroom, which is, of course, the ideal place for a jolly good cry.

Chapter 15

Saturday came. In some ways it was a blessed relief because Jess wouldn't be cooped up in the same schoolroom as Fred all day. But on the other hand, there were things being organised for the weekend – fun things, involving Fred – which normally would have been the highlight of her week.

'Are you going to Pete Collins's party?' Flora had asked, as they parted the previous evening. 'Sounds like fun.'

Pete, a boy in their class with big ears and a happy grin, was celebrating his sixteenth birthday with a murder mystery evening at a posh hotel called the Abercrombie. It was situated in leafy grounds and from the road it looked slightly haunted in a Rocky Horror Mansion kind of way.

'I don't know . . .' Jess hesitated. She knew Fred

was going since she'd had to watch Jodie 'forcing' him to agree. Jodie would, of course, be there – she'd already described the red velvet dress she'd be wearing, which, she warned, 'makes me look like a fat heifer'. Jess's heart sank.

'Jack wants to go,' Flora had admitted. 'You know Pete's brother, Sean, is his mate . . .'

'I might.'

Jess just couldn't decide. It sounded brilliant – she'd always wanted to go to a murder mystery event – but could she face the sight of Jodie flirting like mad with Fred all evening, and Fred just being hustled along and seeming to not mind very much?

'I don't know if I can face it,' said Jess. 'I might have to get a headache. I'll call you tomorrow, OK?'

'OK,' agreed Flora. 'I have to spend all day helping my mum reorganise the house. Nightmare!'

So when she woke up on Saturday morning (still sharing Mum's bed – Jess hoped that blabbermouth Flora hadn't told anyone about *that*), Jess had a big decision to make. Should she go to Pete's party or not? She liked Pete – he was a happy kind of guy. But Pete wasn't the issue: it was Fred. If Fred hadn't been going, Jess would have leaped at the chance to attend a murder mystery evening. It would be a great opportunity to have fun, lose herself in some games and forget all about Fred for an hour or two. But knowing Fred was going to be there sort of dominated the whole thing. And the fact that Fred was going to be there, evidently not caring if she was there or not . . .

By the time she got downstairs, Mum and Dad had had their breakfast and gone out. Granny was doing some baking.

'They've gone to look at a possible flat-share for your dad,' said Granny. 'It's a big house over by the park. I expect you're looking forward to getting your room back, love.'

Jess nodded and got herself a bowl of cereal.

'Saturday!' beamed Granny. 'Best day of the week, eh? What are your plans for tonight?'

'Well, I've been invited to a murder mystery party,' admitted Jess dolefully.

'What?' cried Granny in delight. 'How lovely, dear! I've always wanted to go to one of those. You must tell me all about it and take some photos on your mobile, too.'

'The thing is,' said Jess reluctantly, 'I don't think I'm going to go.'

'Why ever not?' asked Granny. 'It sounds absolutely

brilliant. I'd go myself if I thought I could pass for sixteen again.'

Suppressing a shudder at the thought of going to the murder mystery party accompanied by her grandma, Jess toyed idly with a spoonful of cereal and wondered just how much of her present situation she could share with Granny, who often had a wacky and life-enhancing take on Jess's trials and tribulations.

Just as she was opening her mouth to start on the painful aftermath of the Fred Separation Saga, the front doorbell rang.

'I'll get it!' Jess jumped up because Granny's hands were covered with flour. As she walked down the hall, Jess could make out a shape through the frosted glass of the door and she could tell, because it wasn't a very tall shape, that it wasn't Fred. Fred was over six feet tall now. Cursing herself for even thinking that Fred might be calling to see her, Jess opened the door and was confronted by a total stranger.

It was a middle-aged man with dark, greying hair and big mournful eyebrows. But he had a friendly smile and a soft voice.

'I'm sorry to disturb you,' he said, 'but there's a bird trapped in your garden shed.'

Jess's mind reeled for a moment. Who was this? A

random madman? How did he know what was in their garden shed? She hesitated, puzzled.

'Sorry!' the man went on. 'My name's Quentin Appleton – I've just moved in next door. We were out in our garden storing a few boxes in our shed, when Luke noticed there was a fluttering noise on the other side of the fence.'

'Oh thanks!' gasped Jess. This guy was their new neighbour. 'I'm Jess. Jess Jordan. Hi! Are you settling in OK?'

'Oh yes, thank you. This is perfect for us,' said Mr Appleton. 'We've just moved down from Manchester because I've got a job at St Benedict's.' The guy was a teacher! That could be weird!

'I'll go and let the bird out, then,' said Jess awkwardly. 'It won't panic and fly into my hair, will it?'

'No, I shouldn't think so,' said Mr Appleton. 'But Luke can nip over the fence and let it out for you, if you like.'

'Oh, would he? Thanks,' said Jess. 'I'm not at my best with fluttery things. I'll come and watch, though.'

'Right, then,' said Mr Appleton briskly. 'I'll see you out the back.'

'What's going on?' asked Granny as Jess sped through the kitchen.

'It was the man next door,' said Jess. 'The new people. Mr Appleton.'

'Oh, I've met him,' said Granny. 'He seems quite clever, don't you think? Apparently he's the new Head of Sixth Form at St Benedict's. Don't mention his wife!' She delivered this warning in a kind of hectic hiss.

Unmentionable wife? Head of Sixth Form? Though Mr Appleton wasn't especially tall or fierce-looking, Jess was already slightly afraid of him, but definitely intrigued. She pulled on her fleece and went out into the back garden.

Two heads were looking over the fence. One was Mr Appleton, and the other was a teenage boy with curly fair hair and a shy smile.

'This,' said Mr Appleton, 'is my son Luke. Luke, this is Jess.'

'Hi,' said Jess, slightly distracted by the mad flapping against the shed window.

'Hi,' said Luke. 'I think it's a blackbird.'

Chapter 16

'Get over the fence, Luke,' said Mr Appleton. 'Jess isn't at her best with birds.'

Luke gave his father an odd sideways smile.

'Bad news,' he said, almost as an aside.

Jess didn't know what he meant by this, but he gave her a friendly look as he vaulted over the fence, opened the shed and released the bird, which flew off over the rooftops.

'I wonder how long it was in there?' he mused, looking inside the shed. Jess peeped inside, too.

'Oh, not long, I shouldn't think,' she said. 'Dad was tidying the shed just yesterday.'

'It's probably nesting,' said Mr Appleton, peering over the fence. 'If you leave the window slightly open, then it could get in and out – unless your parents don't want the mess . . . ?'

Jess thought for a minute and pulled a wry face. 'My dad's the tidy one, but he does love birds,' she said. 'He used to spend all his time painting seagulls.'

'Lucky man!' cried Mr Appleton. 'That's what I call a lifestyle!'

There was a short pause and Jess had the feeling that everybody wanted the conversation to continue, but that nobody was quite sure what to say.

'So what does your father do now, Jess?' asked Mr Appleton.

'He's just got a job as a postman,' said Jess. 'He's an artist really, but of course he can't live on that. He's just moved up from Cornwall – he used to live in St Ives.'

'St Ives! Terrific!' smiled Mr Appleton. Even when he was smiling, his eyebrows still looked mournful. 'We had a great holiday there last year, didn't we, Luke? Luke learned to surf.'

'Did you?' Jess now had an excuse to look at Luke again.

He was good-looking, taller than his father, with light green eyes, high cheekbones and fair curly hair blowing about in the wind. His eyebrows weren't mournful – instead they looked kind of energetic. Presumably he had inherited his looks from his unmentionable mother.

'I did do a bit of surfing, yeah,' he said. 'It was great. Do you surf?'

'Only on the internet!' laughed Jess. 'I'm not very sporty, I'm afraid. Whatever I'm doing, my feet always get in the way.'

'Whose are those tennis rackets, then?' Luke looked inside the shed, where various pieces of debris were being kept until they disintegrated completely. It seemed a bit cheeky of him to look in there and make remarks about their sad old possessions, but of course talking to strangers is always a bit awkward.

'They're my mum's,' Jess explained. 'She doesn't really play any more. She's a librarian now.'

'And your granny lives with you, too, doesn't she?' asked Luke's dad. 'I had a word with her yesterday. She said your father is staying at the moment so it's all a bit crowded.'

'That's right.' Jess was slightly unnerved that Granny had discussed the intimate details of their family life, but Mr Appleton seemed impeccably polite. 'Mum and Dad have gone out house-hunting today – well, looking for somewhere for him. It'll be great having him living close by.'

'Yes, St Ives is a long way away, isn't it?' Mr Appleton nodded thoughtfully. There was a brief pause, then he continued, 'Look, Jess, would you and your granny like to come round to lunch today? We could pick your brains about the area – you could tell us where the best surfing is and so on.'

'Surfing?' Jess hesitated. The nearest sea was fifty miles away.

'Just a little joke,' said Mr Appleton with a smirk. 'Sorry. I make Luke cringe twenty-five times a day.'

'More like five thousand,' said Luke, but he looked at his father with quite an affectionate smile.

'I think Granny's going out to lunch with her friend Deborah,' said Jess uncertainly. 'But I'd love to come.'

'Well, just pop round when you're ready, then,' said Mr Appleton. 'We're not doing anything special. Just unpacking.'

'Oh, well . . .' Jess smiled. 'All right. Thanks. I'd love to.'

Mr Appleton beamed. 'It won't be anything much, I'm afraid,' he said. 'We haven't really sorted the kitchen out yet. Come on, then, Luke!'

Luke vaulted back over the fence. Jess wished for a moment that she was lithe and sporty instead of dumb and porky.

'Granny!' she hissed, once she was back inside. 'They've invited me to lunch!'

'Oh, lovely, dear,' bumbled Granny. 'I'm just making cheese scones. You can take some round there if you like. I'm taking a few for Deborah, too.'

'Divine!' cried Jess. 'Thanks, Granny. Now I've gotta get ready!'

She thundered upstairs and confronted herself in the bathroom mirror. Jess knew very well that a thick layer of make-up would be completely inappropriate, but she applied it nevertheless, which took about twenty minutes, and then she cleaned it all off and scrutinised her face in its bare and naked state.

Her eyebrows were OK because she worked on them on a daily basis. Her skin was lightly dotted with spots, but currently there was nothing too monstrous. She'd had a spot on her chin once which had looked like something out of a horror movie – a giant flashing mushroom. She had literally felt it pulsating. But now there was just the usual pink galaxy and Jess plastered it with concealer. The trouble was, the concealer was kind of obvious. What she needed was a product which would conceal the concealer.

Concealer was fine after dark, but in broad daylight, sometimes it just made things look worse. Jess cleaned off the concealer. A mountain of cotton-wool balls was accumulating in the bathroom waste basket.

What a waste of money! She decided that just a hint of eyeliner and lippy would be enough. She chose brown eyeliner – she didn't want to look like a goth. Anyway, there was no need to panic. It was just a meeting-the-neighbours scenario, right?

At half past twelve she put a few cheese scones in a plastic box. Granny had already left for Deborah's. For a split second Jess was overwhelmed by a wave of intense shyness and wished that Granny had been able to come, too. But Jess had to go on her own and in a way she was looking forward to it.

'Hello!' cried Quentin Appleton, welcoming her in with hearty friendliness. Jess looked around. Boxes were everywhere, some half-unpacked, some empty. There was a delicious smell.

'I brought these.' Jess offered the plastic box. 'Cheese scones. My granny made them.'

'Oh, how very kind!' cried Mr Appleton, receiving them with rapture. He opened the box and inhaled deeply. 'Cheese! Wonderful! Come into the kitchen, Jess. Luke's just finishing the minestrone. These scones will go perfectly with it – much better than boring old bread.'

In the kitchen the table had been laid for three, so presumably father and son completed the family group, today at least. Luke had his back to her – he was stirring something on the hob. As she entered, he turned, and a sunbeam caught his eyelashes. He smiled at her.

'I hope you like minestrone,' he said.

'Luke is an enthusiastic cook,' Mr Appleton said, beaming.

'Wow! You're so talented!' Jess felt a little rush of courage. If she could begin to tease Luke, that would make the occasion easier. 'Surfing, cooking, jumping over fences . . .'

'Minestrone's easy,' said Luke a bit bashfully. 'You just sort of chuck in anything that's lying around.'

'I sometimes think that's where I'll end up,' said Mr Appleton with a strange gloomy face. 'In his minestrone!'

'That's another of Dad's little jokes,' smiled Luke. He turned back to the soup, tore a few handfuls of basil up and tossed them in. 'There's Parmesan on the table. We like to grate our own in.'

'Lovely,' beamed Jess.

Mr Appleton was speedily adding the cheese scones to the feast on the table: ciabatta, olives and ham.

'What a lovely meal!' enthused Jess. 'Maybe you should start a restaurant!'

'Maybe we will,' said Mr Appleton. 'Why not? We could call it Dirty Luke's Den.'

Luke caught Jess's eye for a moment and she instantly understood his look. It was a Please Tolerate My Weird Dad look.

She grinned in acknowledgement. 'Great name!' she gushed. 'That should bring the customers in.'

Luke ladled the soup into warm bowls and Jess felt enveloped by happiness. Her favourite tastes and smells were set out before her: tomato, cheese, basil, olives.

'Luke got interested in cooking last summer on our holiday in Italy,' said Mr Appleton.

'Italy!' cried Jess. 'I've always wanted to go there.'

'Luke took some amazing photos,' said Mr Appleton, offering her the Parmesan and a grater. 'He can show you after lunch.'

'Brilliant!' beamed Jess.

'So, Jess.' Mr Appleton picked up his spoon with a very friendly smile. 'Tell us all about yourself!'

Chapter 17

Help, thought Jess. *This is like a job interview*. She knew her only hope of saying anything at all was to get back into comedy.

'Oh! Me,' she sighed, 'I'm just the dull little girl next door – by day, obviously. By night I grow fangs and fly about looking for nice juicy necks.'

'I knew you were one of us!' beamed Mr Appleton.

Jess felt a horrid little shiver run down her spine. There *was* something slightly spooky about those mournful eyebrows of his. There was nothing spooky about Luke's looks, though – with his fair curly hair and green twinkly eyes, he was more like a character out of a Jane Austen story.

'Don't tell Jess all our secrets, Dad,' he said, smiling.

'So what does your mum do, Jess?' asked Mr Appleton.

'By day she's a librarian,' said Jess.

'But by night she's an enemy agent?' suggested Luke.

'You got it!' laughed Jess. 'She's like a baddy from a Bond film, all blood-red nail varnish and cruel eyebrows. The job in the library is just a cover.'

'And what about your granny?' asked Mr Appleton. 'Is she M?'

'She's the mastermind, yes,' said Jess. 'She's had a lifelong interest in homicide. She cut her teeth on Agatha Christie.'

'Tasty!' said Luke.

Jess began to think these neighbours might be quite fun, with their weird jokes and catchphrases. She decided to turn the tables on them and produce some questions of her own.

'What was Manchester like?' she asked.

'Oh, wonderful, of course,' said Mr Appleton. 'But we began to feel we wanted a change.'

Luke seemed to go quiet suddenly and stared darkly at his soup. This must be something to do with the unmentionable mother. Was she dead? In jail? Had she disappeared? Had Mr Appleton . . . made her disappear? Did his mournful eyebrows have an edge of guilt? Had she been intensely irritating? Maybe he'd approached her one day in the garden, secateurs poised, and said, '*My dear, I'd like a word with you*'. And then – *schnak*! He'd pruned her to death.

'Luke misses his mates,' Mr Appleton went on. 'But I'm sure he'll make lots of new friends at St Dominic's. Where do you go to school, Jess?'

'Ashcroft,' Jess informed him. 'We have a great football team, but otherwise we're famous for being rather badly behaved on buses.'

'Do you know anybody at St Dominic's?' asked Mr Appleton.

'Uh, no, I don't think so,' said Jess. 'But I can introduce Luke to all my friends.'

Luke looked up from his minestrone, and a faint expression of curiosity flitted across his face.

'That would be fantastic!' cried his dad. 'Wouldn't it, Luke?'

'Yeah, great,' said Luke. 'So where do you and your mates hang out?'

'At the Dolphin Cafe,' said Jess, 'just off the high street, right round the corner from the town hall. We sometimes go there after school and always at weekends. Saturday and Sunday mornings, everybody hangs out there.'

'But you didn't go today?' asked Mr Appleton.

Jess felt herself blush. 'No, I had stuff to do at home,' she said, hating the blushing and wishing it would stop. She wasn't going to tell the Appletons all about her dreadful bust-up with Fred – the real reason she hadn't turned up at the Dolphin. 'I've been promising my mum all week to do some internet stuff for her. Her PC's in a terrible state – she doesn't save stuff in folders or anything.'

'But I thought she was a librarian.' Mr Appleton looked puzzled. 'Aren't they always very tidy?'

'Mum's got an untidy streak,' said Jess. 'I think she has two sides to her character. She's a bit of a Jekyll and Hyde.'

'As well as a secret agent?' mused Mr Appleton. 'She sounds interesting.'

'Yeah. I'll take you to the Dolphin soon, Luke, if you like,' said Jess, 'and introduce you to the gang.'

'Thanks,' said Luke, with a warm twinkly smile. 'I'd really appreciate that. I feel such a nerd, not having anywhere to go on a Saturday night.'

'Hey! Wait!' A huge idea unfolded in Jess's mind. 'Pete Collins is having a party tonight – a murder mystery party. Would you like to come?'

'But . . .' Luke hesitated. 'I haven't been invited . . .'

'You can go as my guest!' Jess assured him. This

was a brilliant idea. It meant she could go to the party without feeling sidelined by Fred. It was odd, suddenly focusing back in on her life. Being with the Appletons today, she hadn't thought about Fred at all for a while. It was a shock, remembering all that mess. It made her realise how much she'd been obsessing over it. 'Don't worry,' she assured Luke. 'Pete will be cool about it. I'll text him and tell him I'm bringing you.'

'Well . . .' Luke looked really pleased. 'Well, thanks.'

After lunch Mr Appleton went out, and Luke asked Jess for some advice on how to organise his room. It was full of cardboard boxes and the only part of the room in any kind of order was his desk, where his laptop stood, and above the desk, his bulletin board.

'Hey, that's funny!' said Jess. 'My room is just the other side of that wall, and I've got my desk right there in the same place!'

'We can tap out secret messages to each other in Morse code,' said Luke. 'Like in the olden days before texting and email.'

'Or send carrier pigeons,' added Jess. 'Low carbon emissions, obviously, for eco brownie points.'

Luke laughed. 'You're so funny!' he said.

Jess felt pleased that he seemed to rate her modest wit, but she looked away and studied his bulletin board. There were already loads of photos pinned up there: Luke and his mates messing about, wrestling, dressed as pirates – all the usual stuff.

'You must really miss your mates,' she said thoughtfully.

'Yes,' admitted Luke. 'But my friend Boris is coming down next weekend. That's him.' He pointed out a plump-looking boy with very short hair. 'He's really cool. Really clever. We make films together. He's really, really, really going to like you.'

'Me?' Jess was slightly embarrassed.

'Yeah. Hasn't anyone ever told you you look a bit Italian?' Luke looked down at her with what seemed to be a totally authentic smile, as if he meant it.

'Italian?' laughed Jess. 'No way! I'm not the Mediterranean type. I'm typically English with lash-ings of spots and cellulite.'

'Well, I think you'd look great on the big screen.' Luke went on looking at her in a way which made Jess feel slightly uncomfortable. His eyes seemed large and shiny. 'So would you like to be in our next film?'

'Film?' gasped Jess. This was getting better and better.

'We're going to start it next weekend. It's a kind of moody, postmodern, slightly edgy thing about a guy who's haunted by the ghost of his previous girlfriend who died in a car crash.'

'So I'd basically be playing a dead person?' asked Jess with a frisson of disgust and delight.

'A glamorous ghost,' said Luke. 'Lots of white make-up. I can see you looking beautiful against a cloudy sky. Standing under a bridge by the canal . . .'

'Which canal?' asked Jess.

'We'll find one,' said Luke, getting enthusiastic and waving his arms about. 'If there isn't one, we can buy one!'

'Maybe I should practise the look by going to the murder mystery party tonight as a ghost!' mused Jess.

'Yeah!' exclaimed Luke. 'Brilliant! We can both go as ghosts! I've got loads of make-up and capes and things!'

'Wait!' Jess pulled back. 'What if nobody else there is in fancy dress? I mean, if we were the only people dressed as ghosts, it would be weird.'

Luke looked crushed. Jess felt sorry for him – she

hated to stamp on his ideas so early in their relationship.

'I'll call Pete,' she decided, pulling out her mobile. 'I'm sure it'll be cool.'

Chapter 18

'Yeah, great,' said Pete. 'Everybody's coming as zombies and stuff. Bring your mate – bring anybody!'

So Jess and Luke began their transformation into ghosts. Luke started to unpack various boxes which contained his film gear – costumes, make-up, even some weird wigs.

'I'm still such a kid when it comes to dressing up,' he confessed, diving into a long blonde wig for a moment and striking a carnival pose.

Jess had hysterics. Maybe Luke was gay. That would be ace – she had always wanted a Gay Best Friend.

Eventually she nipped home to get her own make-up kit. She wasn't going to give herself up to Luke's make-up in case it was manky in some way. OK, he seemed like a great guy, but she wasn't going to let an almost complete stranger smear stuff on her face.

'Let's get some ideas from the internet,' said Luke, flipping open his laptop when she returned from her house. 'What route shall we go down? Zombies are great, aren't they?'

'Too much gore?' Jess was a bit doubtful. 'I mean, I love zombie movies, but all that blood and bruising and stuff – it would take us ages to do.'

'Hey!' grinned Luke. 'Speaking of zombies, why don't you keep one in your garden shed instead of a blackbird?'

'Yeah!' Jess laughed. 'Wouldn't it be great to have zombies nesting in there? The babies would be really cute! We could take them for a walk in the park!'

'Nice idea!' Luke agreed. 'On leads, with studded collars like pit bull terriers!'

Jess giggled as she imagined the scenario. It felt good to be laughing again – she hadn't been amused much recently.

Luke searched all the ghost and supernatural sites, which used up about two hours, and they ventured into some very spooky territory.

'Thank goodness it's daylight!' shivered Jess, looking behind her. 'This is really freaking me out!'

Luke consulted his watch. 'Hey!' he said. 'Time we

got going! I still favour zombies or vampires. What about you?'

'Vampires are way cooler,' said Jess. 'Zombies are so last season.'

'OK,' nodded Luke. 'You'd look better as a vampire anyway. It would be a waste making you up as a zombie.' He gave her a very direct look.

'What do you mean?' cried Jess, embarrassed.

Luke looked away and rubbed his hands together as if he was thinking about something else. 'Oh, you know,' he said, with a hint of awkwardness. 'Vampires can be kind of glamorous and charismatic, but zombies will always just be gross.' He looked up at her, with a bright smile.

'I'll take that as a compliment, then!' said Jess, keeping it light. 'Fangs a lot!'

'I've got some fangs in here somewhere.' Luke dived into one of the cardboard boxes and rummaged about. Soon they had a set of fangs each, a couple of black velvet cloaks and high white collars.

'I've got a black top I can wear underneath,' said Jess, 'and footless tights. And black suede boots!'

'You'll look the business!' exclaimed Luke. 'Go and get them and we can start our make-up.'

'We should have a snack first,' said Jess. 'My tum

says it's teatime. Come on over and try my granny's cakes – they're amazing. And there might be some cheese scones left.'

'I'd prefer blood scones, but thanks anyway,' said Luke. 'I'll wear my cloak, I think. Just to get in the mood.'

He rammed his fangs back in his mouth, and they raced round to Jess's house.

'Help, help, Granny!' yelled Jess playfully as they thundered in. 'I'm being chased by a vampire!'

There was no sign of anybody – no one was home.

'Oh dear, what an anticlimax.' Jess shrugged. 'Hey, why don't you sit down and I'll get us a toasted sand-wich. Or would you prefer a ciabatta?'

'Ciabatta is betta – bu-boom!' grinned Luke, twirling round in his cape. He knocked a glass off the draining board, and it shattered on the floor. 'Oh no! I'm so sorry!' he exclaimed, looking dismayed. 'I'm so clumsy! Have you got a dustpan and brush? I'll replace it, of course.'

'Goodness gracious, you're so polite!' said Jess with a smile. 'Relax! Don't worry about the glass – it's only a cheap one from the supermarket.' She handed him the dustpan and brush. 'If you sweep up the bits, I'll get cracking with the ciabatta – cheese and tomato OK?'

'Brilliant!' said Luke. 'Thanks so much!' He

crawled around on the floor, sweeping up all the bits, then he found a piece of paper to wrap them in and asked Jess for an old cornflake packet, put the wrapped shards of glass inside it and bound the whole thing up tightly with sticky tape.

Jess watched, amazed. 'Why go to all that trouble?' she asked.

'Well, we don't want the dustbin men to cut themselves,' said Luke, putting the taped box carefully into the rubbish bin.

'Although, of course, if they do . . .' Jess pulled a vampiric face '. . . we'll suck their blood till they beg for mercy!'

The ciabattas were a success, and halfway through the parents arrived home, Mum first, traipsing into the kitchen and looking tired.

Luke jumped to his feet and beamed at her. She looked startled.

'This is Luke from next door,' said Jess. 'This is Mum . . . and Dad.'

'How do you do?' asked Luke confidently, offering a hand to shake.

Mum looked disorientated but faintly charmed by this display of good manners. 'Fine, thank you,' she said hesitantly.

'She's not really fine,' said Dad, edging into the kitchen. 'She's exhausted and she's got a headache. We looked at six different flats, but we did find a good one in the end.'

'And guess what?' Mum added. 'The landlord is Alison's brother – you know, my friend Alison at work – and because the flat's empty, he says Dad can move in right away!'

'Brilliant! Well done!' beamed Jess. 'You must be shattered.'

'Oh, please, sit down!' Luke offered Mum his chair. 'Can I get you a cup of tea?' He headed for the kettle and filled it.

Mum did sit down and exchanged a puzzled glance with Jess, unused to a young person taking such initiative. It was odd to be offered a cup of tea in your own home by a total stranger, but Luke was totally into it and he found the tea, the mugs, the milk – everything.

'It looks a bit odd, you making the tea with you wearing that velvet cloak,' said Mum with an amused glint in her eye.

'Oh, yes, sorry.' Luke smiled apologetically. 'I don't always dress like this – we were thinking of going to a murder mystery party as vampires.'

'I thought you said you didn't want to go to that?'

Mum asked Jess, with a shrewd look.

'I've decided to go,' said Jess sweetly. 'I might have gone anyway, and I can introduce Luke to the gang now.'

'Great idea,' said Dad. 'He and Fred will get on like a house on fire.'

'Who's Fred?' asked Luke, smiling in an encouraging way while setting out mugs and milk on the table.

There was a sudden sickening pause, and Jess felt her face fire up with a burning blush. She glared briefly at her dad before turning to Luke with a gracious smile. 'Just one of the gang,' she said firmly. 'A bit of a comedian.'

'He sounds great!' said Luke. 'I can't wait to meet him!'

Jess wasn't looking forward quite so much to that little introduction.

Chapter 19

Luke's father gave them a lift to the party. They were vampired up to the nines with whitened faces, deadly fangs, scary eyebrows and black eyeliner.

'Have fun and don't go near any mirrors!' said Mr Appleton merrily as they got out of the car.

The Abercrombie Hotel was looking even more atmospheric than usual in the early evening darkness, its huge arched windows and pinnacled roof towering majestically above them.

'Wow!' breathed Luke, staring up in awe. 'I could roost up there, next to that chimney!'

'Great idea!' Jess smiled, but she was beginning to feel nervous. It was only a matter of moments until she'd be confronted with Fred. It was odd that she was with this strange boy – odd, but perhaps helpful. What would Fred think? And what was Fred thinking *right now*? What if he wasn't thinking about her at all? He'd given the impression, recently, that he couldn't care less. He had her email address. He could very easily text her. But he hadn't done any of these things. Far from performing some heroic feat to win her back, he hadn't even lifted a finger.

'Hey! Are you OK?' Luke was staring down at her in concern.

'Oh, sorry!' Jess recovered herself. 'I just remembered something I have to do back home. It's nothing. Come on, let's make our entrance.'

Luke took her arm and they strode together up the wide stone stairs. The fact that he'd taken her arm wasn't important, thought Jess. It was just a theatrical gesture to make the entrance more grand or something. Or maybe Luke himself felt a little nervous and linking arms made him feel more confident. Jess was a little uneasy about it, but she didn't want to make a big thing of it and wriggling away would be ridiculous. She just had to kind of inwardly ignore the fact that they were arm in arm.

The lobby was full of people in evening dress – black tie, ball gowns. Some of them looked across in curiosity as the two vampires entered. Some smiled, some frowned. Jess couldn't see a single person she knew, and besides, they were all middle-aged.

'Excuse me,' she faltered, addressing the nearest woman, 'is this Pete's party?'

The woman smiled in a rather patronising way. 'No,' she purred. 'This is Eleanor and Oscar's engagement party.'

'What?' Jess began to panic. 'What's happened? Have I got it wrong?'

'Ask at reception,' suggested the women, nodding towards a desk where a pale, brooding young man was checking some documents.

'I reckon he's one of us,' whispered Luke as they approached. 'The fangs have been withdrawn until he's off duty.'

Jess giggled slightly, but she was beginning to feel really panicked. Where had Pete's party gone? 'Excuse me,' she said. 'We're looking for Pete Collins's murder mystery party . . . ?'

'It's in the Tennyson Suite,' murmured the receptionist, his dark eyes flickering over their vampire costumes. 'Down the hall and turn right.'

As they burst into the Tennyson Suite there was a much more cheerful hubbub of teenage voices, both raucous and shrill.

'Jess!' squealed somebody. It was Flora, waving from the far end.

Instantly Jess saw that Fred was standing over on the right, beside an enormous fireplace, and Jodie and a few others were with him. Jodie was wearing a close-fitting red clingy dress. She looked amazing.

But Jess had a worse discovery to make: as she looked around the room, she saw that nobody else was in fancy dress. There were no vampires, no zombies, no skeletons, no ghouls. Everybody, but everybody, was smart casual – or smarter.

'Oh no!' gasped Jess. 'We're the only people in fancy dress! Pete promised me there'd be zombies wall to wall!'

'Never mind,' said Luke. 'All the more blood for us!'

Jess laughed faintly.

Flora was approaching with Ben Jones and Mackenzie, and Jodie noticed them, too, and came bounding up. Fred stayed by the fire and pretended not to have seen them. Jess clearly saw the moment when he didn't see them, even though she wasn't even looking at him herself. He turned his back and pretended to warm himself by the blazing logs.

'Jess!' screamed Jodie. 'You look amazing! But why have you come in fancy dress? And who's your handsome friend? Aren't you going to introduce us?'

'This is Luke,' said Jess. 'Luke, this is Jodie, and Flora, and Ben and Mackenzie.'

Everybody smiled and admired their costumes, but Jess felt slightly furious that they were the only ones dressed weirdly.

'So where have you come from?' Jodie asked Luke.

'I've come from my coffin,' Luke informed her. 'And I've got my eye on your neck.'

Jodie screamed in delight.

Suddenly it occurred to Jess that if Jodie and Luke hit it off, it would be quite helpful in the present circumstances. Luke's strange bold manner and confident ways might turn Jodie's head and distract her from her growing attachment to Fred.

'Yes, Jodie is famous for her delicious neck,' Jess said encouragingly. 'It's got five-star feedback on the vampires' website.'

'I must try it, then!' exclaimed Luke. Seizing Jodie, he then plunged his face into her neck.

Flora, Ben and Mackenzie looked a bit surprised because Luke was acting as if he'd known them for ever – as if he was already one of the gang.

'Mmmm!' Luke emerged from Jodie's neck. 'Type O, I think. A pleasant fruit bouquet and full-bodied aftertaste.'

'Full-bodied is right,' said Mackenzie mischievously.

Jodie slapped him playfully across the shoulder.

'Keep your trap shut, shorty!' she snapped.

Pete Collins then approached, accompanied by a woman aged about thirty and wearing a smart black dress.

'Pete!' wailed Jess. 'You told us everybody was coming dressed as zombies and stuff!'

'Sorry!' beamed Pete. 'We must have got our wires crossed.' He gave her a naughty wink. So that was it! Pete had set her up. It was hard to be cross with him, though, because he was a cheery, happy kind of guy, and besides, it was his birthday.

'Happy birthday, then, you idiot!' said Jess.

'Thanks,' said Pete. 'This is Jemma – she's organising the murder mystery.'

'Hello!' said Jemma. 'What lovely costumes! You do look wonderful! But I just wanted to say that for the murder mystery to work properly, everyone has to cooperate and follow instructions. So although you're dressed as vampires, we don't want any free-range biting and sucking and stuff, OK?'

'No, no,' said Jess politely. 'Of course not!' She wouldn't dream of undermining Pete's party, though she didn't rule out the possibility that she might pull his ears sometime next week as revenge for making her come in fancy dress.

'Right!' agreed Luke. 'Although, if I may say so, you have a remarkably tempting neck!'

Jemma looked uneasy and faintly disgusted. Jess began to feel the tiniest frisson of uncertainty. Could she trust Luke to behave and cooperate? There was something about his energy and confidence which meant she wasn't sure what he might do next. And they hadn't even properly encountered Fred yet.

Chapter 20

'Right,' said Jemma in a businesslike way, 'here are your character cards. From now on you'll be in character, OK? The card gives you your persona for this evening and you'll be mingling with other guests in character. We're serving nibbles and drinks now, then there'll be an event, then we'll go on to the main buffet and after that there'll be the interrogations.'

'Luke,' whispered Jess urgently, 'I think we should take our fangs out. This card says I'm a bank clerk called Felicity Finance.'

'What a shame!' sighed Luke. 'I was really getting into it. It gives you carte blanche to bite the necks of attractive girls.' He whipped his fangs out and put them in his pocket.

'I think we should get rid of the cloaks, too.' Jess was anxiously wriggling out of hers, but somehow her arm got stuck in the lining and instantly Luke was helping her – he had such perfect manners. 'We still have the scary white faces, though.' Jess, still struggling with her trapped arm, knew she would feel very self-conscious even without her cloak and fangs. Why oh why had they ever got into this stupid vampire scene?

'Don't worry,' Luke assured her. 'You look ravishing.' He gently disentangled her, pulling her arm out of the folds of cloth.

'Hi!' The word came like a bullet from behind her left shoulder. Jess twisted round awkwardly to find a figure standing, watching. It was Fred, a mocking expression on his face. The suddenness of his appearance caught her off guard.

'Oh, Luke –' she stumbled and mumbled. 'This is, er, Fred.'

'No it isn't,' Fred contradicted her. 'I am Sir William Gobion, fresh from an expedition to the Andes, where I contracted a fatal disease – wait, I wasn't supposed to tell you that.'

'Great to meet you,' said Luke, giving Fred a firm handshake. 'Sorry to hear about the fatal disease – hope you have travel insurance. I'm . . . Ah! I'm Cyrus S. Spoonfinger, a slightly shady insurance salesman from New York. Though perhaps I shouldn't have told you that I was slightly shady.'

'Don't worry! Don't worry!' Fred was finding his way into his English gentleman character with a booming voice. 'I prefer deep shade. And besides, you're an American – that's all that matters. If you're going to murder me, I know you'll do it fair and square with one of your lovely American guns.'

Luke chuckled. 'But if *you're* going to murder *me*,' he replied, 'it could be with something nasty you've brought back from the Andes.' He turned to Jess. 'Don't accept finger food from this man! What's your name again, ma'am?'

Jess was beginning to feel a bit left out as Luke and Fred indulged in pre-murder banter.

'Felicity Finance,' she informed them. She knew from her character card that she was deeply involved in swindling the bank out of several thousand a week, but she wasn't sure whether she was supposed to tell anybody that. 'I work in a bank,' she said lamely. This was awful! Being Felicity was no fun at all compared to Sir William Gobion and Cyrus Spoonfinger. But worse than that, she felt paralysed by self-consciousness. Fred had been watching her getting

out of her cloak. He must have seen L......
in that attentive way, untangling her arm ca...
tenderly, almost.

'I'm undergoing species reassignment,' she added swiftly, reaching in desperation for the most preposterous thing she could think of, something so wildly left-field it wouldn't be on anybody's card, ever. She must, *must* appear dazzlingly witty and charming to Fred, not some kind of speechless nerd. It somehow made it worse that Luke was so confident and articulate.

'What species, may I ask, are you going to become?' enquired Fred in his booming Sir William voice. 'I regularly shoot and eat other species, so I'm very pleased to hear it. If you could manage to become a pheasant, or perhaps a deer, that would be excellent news. I could devour you with a lemon and thyme stuffing, which, let's face it, is the best thing that could ever happen to a bank clerk.'

Luke cracked up. He was evidently finding Fred totally hilarious. Jess liked the way Luke didn't feel he had to show off all the time and that he could appreciate Fred's banter. Or she would have liked it if she could have concentrated on it, instead of being so dreadfully aware that since Fred had come over to talk to them, he had seemed completely normal and relaxed, as if nothing was the matter. The fact that he'd come over at all was in itself disconcerting. He should be lurking in a corner of the room, a tormented look clouding his brow. Or he should have picked a fight with Luke and knocked him down.

'I'd like to have species reassignment,' said Luke thoughtfully.

'What would you be?' asked Fred in his posh voice. 'What did you say you were? Some kind of insurance salesman? Then presumably you'd be some kind of disgusting invertebrate.'

'Yes, I think that would be ideal,' grinned Luke. 'A slug, perhaps. I'd like to be able to make girls scream.'

'Oh absolutely!' agreed Fred. 'I've made girls scream in every continent and I can honestly say there's no sport to beat it. Ha, ha!'

Ridiculously, Jess began to feel a tiny bit upset. Obviously it was good that Fred and Luke were getting on well, but it seemed to her that perhaps they were getting on just a little too well somehow – she felt almost excluded.

This was so stupid! After all, they were only interacting in character, it was all just a bit of fun, and

Fred and Luke were both amusing guys, so why wasn't she amused? Why did she feel so moody and self-conscious?

As the evening went on there were delicious canapés and there was, eventually, a 'murder' – poor Mackenzie was the victim.

'Great choice of victim!' Jess whispered to Luke. 'Mackenzie lying still and saying nothing for the rest of the evening is almost an impossibility!'

Luke laughed. 'I like that friend of his – what's his name? Ben,' he said. 'I think he's got the hots for you, by the way.'

'Oh, no, no, no!' laughed Jess. 'I used to have the hots for him way back, then I got over it, and we did try dating once, but it didn't work.' She'd been going to say, '*I was totally wrapped up in Fred, and it was at a time when Fred and I had had a little tiff*' ... But she didn't want to tell Luke about Fred. It was too private.

Luke had got friendly very quickly, and of course this was good. It would have been dire if he'd been painfully shy, like her poor French exchange partner last year – taking him to school with her and escorting him about had been like carrying around a sack of cement. Luke could take care of himself. He made friends easily, he chatted to her mates and made them laugh. He had also got on brilliantly with Fred. But Jess didn't want Luke to know about her history with Fred.

Eventually the murder was solved, ice-cream sundaes were served and everybody congratulated Pete on a great party. But Jess felt somehow cheated. She'd never been able to relax fully or get into her character properly – something, normally, she'd have absolutely adored. It had been too hard to concentrate. Instead of listening to people's gossip, planning blackmail and working out who were likely suspects by picking up clues, Jess had been tormented by picking up clues in an entirely different scenario.

For the whole evening, Fred had behaved perfectly naturally towards her and Luke. He hadn't shown the slightest hint of jealousy. It was as if their special relationship had never existed. To Jess, the memory of being Fred's girlfriend was so vivid that sometimes she could think of nothing else. She was stuck in a state of mind where she was waiting for Fred to attempt reconciliation. But Fred seemed to have moved on effortlessly, as if being Jess's boyfriend had been nothing so very special after all.

And Jess had been distracted by a really silly preoccupation with Fred and Jodie – every moment of the evening she found herself wondering if they were together. They were quite often near each other during the party, but because of the murder mystery scenario people had to mingle. Were they together in that other, much more significant sense, though? Every time Jodie stood next to Fred she would fling an arm around him, slap his shoulder, or pull his hair, but Jodie was like that with everybody. Was this touchy-feelyness with Fred just Jodie's way, or was it something special?

By the end of the evening Jess felt emotionally shattered, and as they rode home in Mr Appleton's car, she hardly joined in with Luke's babble.

'It was brilliant!' he enthused over and over. 'I can't wait to tell Boris about it. He'll be so jealous! And your friends are amazing, Jess. Thanks so much for the best evening ever!'

Jess smiled weakly, handed back the fangs and cloak, thanked Luke for his company and his dad for the lift, then hauled herself up her front path as if all the cares of the world were on her shoulders. Well, at least she'd done a good deed, introducing Luke to the gang. She was glad *he* had enjoyed the party. For her own part, she felt mysteriously as if she'd spent the evening tied up in a sack with ten bad-tempered pit bull terriers.

Chapter 21

Now she had to face her family, who were all gathered round the kitchen table having a late-night cup of cocoa.

'How was the murder mystery?' asked Granny eagerly. 'I've stayed up specially to hear all about it.'

Jess's heart sank. She could hardly remember much about the murder mystery side of things. All she could remember was the way Fred had been completely and utterly normal – a sight which had driven her towards the edge of insanity as the evening had progressed.

'Oh, normal,' she said in an offhand way.

'What do you mean, normal?' asked Granny, puzzled.

'What's wrong?' asked Mum, instantly noticing something odd about Jess's behaviour.

'Nothing,' said Jess. 'I'm just tired, that's all. I think

I'll go upstairs and take this stupid vampire make-up off.'

'Wait!' cried Dad. 'Aren't you going to tell us all about it? Don't you want a cup of cocoa?'

'No thanks, Dad,' said Jess limply, pausing at the bottom of the stairs. 'I'm so tired. I think I'll just go to bed.'

'How was Luke?' called Mum anxiously.

'Absolutely fine!' Jess replied, dragging herself upstairs. 'Goodnight!'

There was a chorus of *goodnight*s from the kitchen, but Jess could imagine the looks they were giving one another. She knew she was going to face further inter-rogation in the morning. As she lay down on her pillow that night, the smell of make-up remover lingering unpleasantly in her nostrils, she thought sadly about how Fred should have behaved.

Ever since they'd parted on Valentine's Day, she'd been waiting for him to woo her back by doing some-thing terrific, something to prove that he still adored her, something creative and imaginative – after all, he was the most imaginative boy in the world. But he'd done nothing.

Jess reflected sadly that the reason she'd dumped Fred had been that he'd done nothing – that he hadn't helped her to organise the dinner dance, while all the time pretending he was busy with it. Perhaps there was something ultimately spineless about Fred. The fact that he hadn't found a way to tell her he was tormented without her, or begged her to take him back was bad enough – it presumably meant she wasn't all that important to him – but it also meant that Fred wasn't as brilliant and wonderful as she had always thought, that he didn't seize life and make what he wanted of it, that instead he was somehow passive and liable to drift. She really didn't want him to be that kind of person, whether they were together or not.

When Jess went down to breakfast the next day, something unexpected happened. Mum and Dad appeared to have gone out, but Granny looked up from the breakfast table with a mischievous twinkle.

'This letter came mysteriously during the night!' she said excitedly. 'Delivered By Hand.'

Jess's heart gave a huge leap, and she felt herself blush deeply. A white envelope lay on the table beside her place. Her name was written on it, or rather printed in kind of deliberately anonymous block letters. Swiftly she picked it up and ran upstairs. Perhaps this was it, she thought excitedly, her fingers shaking as she locked herself in the bathroom, her heart pounding and kicking like a mad thing. She tore open the envelope and pulled out a sheet of paper. Her heart gave another leap. It was a poem!

Beautiful vampire, you haunt my dreams.
I could salute you with terrible screams,
If you'd only appear at my window at night,
Your fangs nicely dripping, your face ghastly white.
Oh, come to my pillow and take a big bite!

I've been a bit lonely since we said goodbye,
But I know you must hide from the bright sunny sky.
I'll be waiting, blood ready, the moment it's night,
So come, lovely vampire, and give me a fright.

Being Jess-less for ever just isn't an option;
I'd rather put myself up for adoption
By ogres or wolves. I am feeling quite ill,
So, beautiful vampire, appear at my sill.

Jess's heart gave a demented leap. At last Fred had done something to make amends! And how typical of him to do it with a mysterious, anonymous poem delivered in the middle of the night! That was *so* Fred!

But it wasn't really anonymous – Fred's signature humour was all over it. *I've been a bit lonely since we said goodbye* – that was obviously a reference to their bust-up. *Being Jess-less for ever just isn't an option* – well, that was his way of saying he was desperate to get back together again. He'd even used the phrase 'Jess Less' when they'd been having coffee after seeing the Bond film. All those little clues . . . it was so sweet of him, so really, really sweet!

Jess kissed the poem – after all, it was the first time anyone had written her a poem, and it was really romantic despite Fred's usual wry humour peeping out here and there. It was a quite wonderful poem and she would keep it for ever. And when they were old and grey, surrounded by grandchildren, the poem would be hanging on the wall in its frame, faded but still fabulous.

Jess folded it carefully and stashed it away in her bra, next to her heart. Then she bounded downstairs.

'So . . . ?' asked Granny, lifting an enquiring eyebrow. 'Judging by the look in your eye I assume everything's all right now?'

'You can bet your sweet life it is, Granny!' beamed Jess. 'It's going to be French toast for me this morning, with all the trimmings! And the moment I've guzzled all that down I'm going over to Fred's.'

'Ah!' said Granny, smiling fondly. 'All's well that ends well, then, love. I'm so pleased for you.'

Chapter 22

As Jess had slept in late, it was around noon by the time she finally left for Fred's. Of course it had taken an hour to decide what to wear. She'd been tempted to borrow the cloak and fangs from Luke again, so that she could complete the wonderful storybook reconciliation by appearing on Fred's doorstep dressed as the Jess in his poem. But she'd decided it would be too embarrassing to walk through town in fancy dress – it had been bad enough last night when she and Luke had arrived at Pete's party and realised they were the only guests in costume.

After discarding the vampire idea, Jess had tried on approximately five thousand clothing combinations, exploring the concepts of Beach Girl, Vamp, Boho, Jane Austen heroine, Hollywood Minx, Hamlet (white shirt and black leggings are always a turn-on, but Jess came to the conclusion that her legs were too fat for Hamlet) . . .

Eventually she'd decided on the simplest outfit: jeans and a grey top (under her fleece, naturally, as the weather was still quite nippy). A scarf loosely knotted around her neck completed the ensemble. She had seventeen scarves, but after trying them all on, had chosen one of Mum's, a nice, cream, sort of mohair that somehow made her face look softer and more smiley.

Her face had also undergone extensive refurbishment in anticipation of the reunion. She'd tried a dozen different make-up styles on her eyes, but none of them seemed to match her lips, so in the end she'd just gone for a hint of mascara and a slick of lipgloss – after all, it was Sunday morning. One didn't want to look too garish as one trotted past the Methodist church.

And as she did trot past the Methodist church, Jess silently sent up a prayer of heartfelt thanks to God, for gently prompting Fred to write that poem. Presumably it had been God's delightful plan to make them realise how divinely happy they'd been together by subjecting them to misery for a short while. Jess felt that such a great weight had been lifted off her, she practically flew along the pavement.

Thanks so much, God, old bean, you miracle-worker, she thought as she sped along. *To show my gratitude I'll be a good girl from now on and will never shout at Mum again*. This was quite a rash promise, but Jess was determined to show God that his generosity was not wasted on a sinner. *And thanks for creating Fred, by the way*, she added, turning the corner into Fred's street. *He really is one of your masterpieces*.

Now she was at the masterpiece's door. For a second she hesitated, her heart leaping joyously in her chest. It was like first-night nerves in a play – this was the moment she'd been longing for, but she had to compose herself for a moment and savour it.

She rang the bell and Fred's mum answered it. When she saw Jess, her face performed a funny little charade – she looked amazed, delighted, then sort of embarrassed.

'Jess, how nice to see you!' she said, beaming, then she hesitated. She didn't immediately ask Jess in. Of course, Fred's mum must have been as upset about their bust-up as her own parents, and she probably didn't have a clue that this was the sacred day on which everything was going to come right again.

'Lovely to see you, too!' gushed Jess politely. 'How are you? And how is Mr Parsons?'

'Oh, fine, fine, thanks!' replied Mrs Parsons with a friendly smile.

There was a tiny pause, during which Fred's mum still didn't invite Jess in. It must be awkward for her, thought Jess.

'Is Fred in?' she asked boldly. Well, someone had to take the initiative.

'Of course! Come in.' Mrs Parsons stood aside. 'Fred!' she called upstairs, as Jess stepped joyfully over the threshold.

There was the sound of a door opening above.

'Fred!' Mrs Parsons repeated. 'It's Jess!'

Fred appeared on the landing, holding a paintbrush and wearing a paint-spattered shirt over his regular clothes. He looked down at Jess and turned bright red. He was remembering his poem, of course.

'Hi,' he said. 'My room's having a makeover. Come on up! The more the merrier.'

As she bounded up the stairs, something at the back of Jess's mind warned her that 'the more the merrier' was a slightly strange phrase to use. She realised Fred had to say something non-committal in front of his mum. Once they were safely in his bedroom with the door closed, she could throw herself into his arms and give him the biggest hug available outside the bear species. She didn't even care if she got paint stains all over her top!

She entered his room – and suddenly the air seemed to crack in half, because there stood Jodie. For a second Jess's heart stopped, her brains flew out of her ears, her blood boiled, her spit turned to steam and her fingernails fried. This was so totally unexpected and a blinding shock, but she had to turn her astonishment and dismay into something else. They mustn't see how gutted she was.

'This is . . . amazing!' she gasped.

Luckily there was actually plenty to be astonished about. All Fred's furniture was piled up in the middle of the room and covered with a dust sheet. One entire wall had been painted pale blue – previously it had been a kind of ordinary cream. The blue contrasted fetchingly with the bright pink of Fred's face. Even Jodie was blushing a bit. But being Jodie, she fought off any awkwardness and dived straight into self-justification.

'I've been on at Fred to give his bedroom a make-over,' she announced confidently, 'ever since I came and visited him when he had the flu.'

'Ah,' said Jess, somehow refraining from strangling Jodie. In all her time with Fred, she had never once presumed to suggest to him what colour he should paint his bedroom walls. It was almost as if he and Jodie were *engaged* or something. 'Great idea!' she added through gritted teeth. 'I like the blue.'

She hated the blue, actually. She would never wear blue again. If Jodie's eyes had been blue, Jess would have scratched them out just as soon as she'd managed to grow fingernails long enough. Jodie's eyes, fortunately for her, were a kind of hazel colour.

'It's called Shallows,' explained Jodie, admiring her own taste in blue. 'It makes you think of tropical beaches, doesn't it?'

'Shallows is a great name,' remarked Jess sourly. 'As Fred lies here and looks at his walls he can think fondly of all his shallow friends.'

'Fred will always be thinking of me, then!' Jodie declared. 'Because I've got to be the shallowest person he knows! Ha, ha! Hard luck, Jess!'

This horrible speech made Jess's soul shrivel. Jodie was trying, in her ham-fisted way, to turn an awkward situation into something of a fun occasion, but she'd only succeeded in trampling all over Jess's heart and soul.

There was still an uncertainty, in the relationship sense, about what Jodie was doing in Fred's bedroom. OK, she was helping him paint, which was in itself a harmless occupation and didn't necessarily imply that they were an item, but the fact that this was a make-over masterminded by her was seriously bad news. Was Fred being dragged unwillingly into Jodie's powerful orbit? Was the vampire poem a cry for help?

Jess had to find a discreet way of mentioning the poem now, to show Fred she understood that every-thing would be all right again and that they could fall into each other's arms the very minute that pesky Jodie was out of sight.

Chapter 23

'Sorry I can't stay. I'd have loved blue streaks in my hair!' With a desperate effort Jess struggled to recover something like her usual witty banter. 'But I have other things to do. I just dropped by because of a poem.'

Fred looked blank. 'A poem?' he repeated, frowning slightly. Oh no! Of course, he had to pretend he didn't know anything about it in front of Jodie. 'What poem?'

Jess had to change tack, and quickly. Her mind reeled and grabbed at other poetic possibilities. 'I'm writing a poem,' she gabbled hastily. 'About, er, pirates.' It mustn't be a poem about heartbreak, obviously. Shipwreck . . . well, that was a whole other ball game.

'Pirates?' repeated Jodie, as if she was involved in this conversation. 'Why a poem?'

'It's for . . . a competition,' Jess blurted out, drowning in lies.

'What competition?' demanded Jodie. 'What's the prize? Can anybody enter?'

'I forget what the prize is,' snapped Jess. 'I think it's a thousand pounds or something. But the prize isn't important.'

'Of course the prize is important, you dumbo!' yelled Jodie. 'A thousand smackeroos! Quick, where's the entry form? If I can do makeovers, I can write poetry!'

'But what does this sudden interest in poetry have to do with me?' asked Fred. *What indeed?* thought Jess in a desperate spin. Then she had a moment of sheer inspiration.

'Didn't you have a, er, rhyming dictionary?' she spluttered.

'A rhyming dictionary?' Fred looked genuinely puzzled. 'Whatever gave you that idea?'

'Oh no – wait!' Jess slapped her head and staged a fit of remembering. 'It was Flora! Of course! Her sister Freya writes poems all the time! I'll nip off to Flora's, then! Sorry to have gatecrashed your painting party.' She backed away towards the door.

'But you've got to tell me all the details about the poetry competition!' wailed Jodie.

'Tomorrow,' promised Jess, hesitating for a split second by the door. Should she give Fred a last desperate burning look? No, she decided that would be too needy. Instead she gave him a casual light-hearted glance. 'See you at school, people!' she quipped in a Californian accent (to hide her anguish). And then she was down the stairs and out of there.

It seemed colder than when she'd been skipping along the pavement on her way over to Fred's. Crocuses were blooming in all the gardens – a sign of spring, but now they seemed sinister. Flowers were possessed by the devil, Jess decided. They seemed to suggest that the world was a lovely place, whereas really it was vile.

Had Fred written that poem? Was he just pretending not to know what she was talking about? What was he thinking? It was sometimes so hard to know what was going on in Fred's head. Presumably he had in some way fallen under Jodie's spell and felt paralysed, unable to shake her off or say anything meaningful to Jess while Jodie was around.

A bird was singing in a tree nearby, a terrible shrill sound that seemed to penetrate her brain and gave her a headache. *Spring really sucks*, thought Jess. She was so deeply confused, she was halfway to Flora's before she realised she didn't need to go there, because she wasn't really looking for a rhyming dictionary and she wasn't really writing a poem about pirates. Sometimes her lies were so vivid she believed them herself.

She paused beside a flowering hedge. The flowers were red. They looked like gouts of gore from a broken heart.

'Oh stop it, you loser!' she snapped to herself. It was time to take control of her feelings and she might as well go and see Flora – it would be a distraction, at least. Flora would be busy with her own life and Jess had noticed how, when there were other people around, she could forget about the whole Fred mess for hours on end, like when she'd had lunch with Luke and his dad.

As soon as she arrived Flora whisked her upstairs, away from the busy kitchen where Mrs Barclay and Felicity were arguing about something.

'Hmmm . . .' murmured Jess. 'It seems she's reached that awkward age . . .'

'Mum or Felicity?' giggled Flora. It was great to be with Flo again – she always made Jess feel better. 'Come and see my new room,' she went on. 'I can use Freya's room till Easter. My room's got to be the B & B guest bedroom because of the en suite, but I love Freya's because she's got this massive walk-in wardrobe and the sofa!' Flora hurled herself gaily on to the enormous white sofa. She didn't look like someone in the grip of a life crisis.

'Great!' observed Jess.

'Get a load of the built-in wardrobe!' Flora said, grinning happily. Jess ventured in and found a space almost as big as her own bedroom. 'I've chucked all Freya's old stuff into a couple of boxes!' Flora went on gleefully. 'Look at all the room I've got!'

'The wardrobe's almost big enough to rent out to somebody else,' said Jess. 'My dad was looking for somewhere, but he's found a flat now.'

'That would be weird,' giggled Flora, 'having your dad as a lodger in my wardrobe! Still, at least he's more user-friendly than my dad.'

'How is your dad now?' asked Jess gently. 'In fact, how's . . . everything?'

Flora suddenly changed and started to look pensive. 'All right, I think. It's so hard to tell. I never know what he's thinking. Are all men like that?'

'My dad's not,' shrugged Jess. 'We get a moment-by-moment commentary about what my dad's thinking.'

'Yeah, well, your dad's different,' commented Flora with a wry smile. 'So he's found somewhere to live

– that's good. You can get your room back.' She looked sympathetically at Jess, and then her mood seemed to transform into something more thoughtful and subdued.

'It must be really hard for you, giving up your room,' said Jess gently. 'But hey! You've kept your house. And you've got a timeshare in a walk-in wardrobe and a massive sofa. Look – this is bigger than the sofa in our living room.'

'I know, I know. It's fine.' Flora still looked troubled, though, kind of staring at the carpet in a way which suggested deeply negative vibes.

'Try not to let it get to you, Flo,' Jess said, giving a hug. 'I know it's tricky, but you'll get through it. I know you've got a lot to cope with, but you've got a great family, a lovely boyfriend, an adorable dog . . .'

'It's not me I'm worried about,' said Flora, restlessly tugging at the fringe on a cushion.

'Your mum and dad will get through it! You've always told me how your dad adores your mum – he'll get you out of this mess. He's not a quitter.'

'No, no, it's not my parents I'm worried about.' Flora turned to Jess with an anxious face. Her lip was trembling slightly. 'It's you.'

'Me?' Jess was taken aback for a moment. 'Me? Why?'

'Well . . .' Flora looked uneasy. She pulled her feet up on to the sofa, curled up into a tight little ball, bit her lip and stared at the carpet again. 'It's just . . . last night, after you'd gone home, I saw Jodie and Fred wandering around the hotel grounds – and they were holding hands.'

An invisible scorching flame swept through Jess's body, barbecuing her liver. But she couldn't let Flora see how she felt.

'So?' she commented archly. 'It's not a crime.' It was a crime, of course, and she was already planning her revenge, though she wasn't quite sure who she would kill first – Fred or Jodie.

Flora's baby-blue eyes widened in disbelief. 'You . . . don't mind?' she asked falteringly. 'You're . . . OK about it?'

'Why should I care?' Jess shrugged, struggling to suppress a silent scream.

At this point, fortunately perhaps, Flora's mother entered the room. She looked frazzled and not at all as elegant as she used to in the days when lying on the sofa reading magazines was her first priority.

'Flora,' she said, 'I really need your help. Sorry, Jess, but we have loads to do today.'

'It's fine!' Jess leaped off the sofa. Continuing the

conversation with Flora would have been near impossible anyway. Jess wasn't used to hiding her feelings from Flora or telling her white lies. And she felt so utterly boiling with rage that she needed to get into the fresh air and walk home very fast in order to have any hope of exorcising her demons.

Chapter 24

When she arrived home, fortunately only Granny was there. She popped out of her room and greeted Jess with a beaming smile.

'All sorted, then, dear?'

'Not at all,' sighed Jess. 'Fred is – Fred was painting his room with Jodie. I seem to have got my wires crossed.'

'Jodie?' Granny looked indignant. 'Isn't she that chubby girl with the loud voice?'

'Well, she's slimmed down a bit recently,' admitted Jess, 'although she's still fat in all the right places.'

'But that voice!' Granny shook her head. 'He'll soon get tired of her, love. He's probably just trying to make you jealous.'

'I don't think so.' Jess plonked herself down on a kitchen chair. 'He didn't seem particularly pleased to see me, and Flora told me he and Jodie were holding hands after the party last night.' She hadn't meant to go into all this with Granny, but somehow it came tumbling out.

Granny headed for the fridge. 'I've just made some leek and potato soup, dear,' she said. 'Why don't you have a bit? It'll warm you up.'

Jess didn't really want to eat anything, but she didn't have the heart to say no. As Granny bustled about, heating up the soup and setting the table, Jess sat with her head in her hands, staring at the patterns in the wooden tabletop. She had to stop all this moping, pull herself together and move on.

'I don't think holding hands means very much,' said Granny after some thought. 'When I was your age, I was always holding hands with somebody. I can't even remember their names now.'

'Yes, but that was back in the romantic era,' Jess reminded her. 'Holding hands was practically compulsory. Fred hardly ever holds hands with anybody. Up till now I don't think he's held anybody's hand but mine.'

'But that Jodie creature,' said Granny scornfully, 'isn't she a bit, er, pushy? I imagine a lot of people who didn't really want to have held hands with her.'

'That's true,' conceded Jess. 'But it's not very comforting, Granny. Let's talk about something else. How was your morning?'

Granny ladled out the soup and tried to remember how her morning had been. 'Deborah rang to say she's got flu,' Granny confided. 'I feel I ought to go and see her, but I'm afraid I might catch it.'

'But didn't you have the flu jab?' asked Jess, picking up her spoon.

'Oh yes! So I did! So I could take round something nice, couldn't I? I might bake some chocolate brownies – she loves chocolate – and I expect you'd like a little treat at teatime to cheer yourself up, eh, dear?'

'Granny, you are naughty! I told you, I need to lose weight! I did a test on the internet and it said my BMI was 25.8, which is way too high.'

'I thought BMI was a car,' pondered Granny. 'Anyway, take no notice of these silly questionnaires. You're perfect as you are. I'll tell you when I think you're getting obese.'

'It'll be too late by then!' laughed Jess. 'This soup is yummy, though – and it's not bad for me, is it?'

'No, no, dear. Lovely veg, that's all it is, and home-made stock.'

'Full marks, Granny!' smiled Jess. 'You're a hero!'

'Ah, there was something else that happened this morning!' Granny suddenly remembered. 'That boy from next door came round – Leo – no, Luke, isn't it? I told him you were out. I didn't say where you'd gone.' Granny winked mischievously. 'I thought you might want to keep a few irons in the fire!'

'Granny, I don't know what you're driving at!' exclaimed Jess, finishing the soup. She was hardly listening, really. Her annoying brain had gone back to that moment when Flora had seen Fred and Jodie holding hands. She tried to imagine the scene and it made her feel slightly sick.

'Thanks, that was lovely.' Jess got up and washed her bowl. 'I think I'd better go up and get stuck into my homework.'

'Your dad's been moving his stuff over to Fisher Street!' called Granny. 'Isn't it great that Mum knows the landlord so Dad could move in right away! You've got your room back now!'

Jess entered her room. Almost all Dad's stuff had gone and the room looked strangely tidy. She ripped off her fleece and threw it on the floor to give the place that cosy lived-in look. Then she sat down at her desk and got out her school books.

History. Yes. Her history with Fred went back quite

a way. She remembered how they'd got together. There had always been that spark, that banter between them, for years and years. It was only when Flora had told her, ages ago, that she fancied Fred that Jess had realised with the most tremendous crash like a building collapsing that Fred was *hers*, even though at the time she'd been under the impression that she had a crush on Ben Jones. And somehow she and Fred had got together when he'd allowed her to cut his hair. She thought of that moment with great tenderness. She still had a bit of the hair in an envelope in the bottom drawer of her desk. She wasn't going to look at it now, though.

She turned over her school books idly. Geography. She and Fred had had their own special geography, too. In summer, the park had been their perfect place. There was a particular tree – it was a flowering cherry or something – and they'd spent hours under that tree, writing comedy sketches and staring into each other's eyes. He'd made her a daisy chain once, and she'd joked that that was the nearest he'd ever get to giving her jewellery.

She jumped up from her desk. She had to stop thinking like this. She had to escape from all this gloomy nostalgia. Being needy and nerdy was deeply unattractive. She needed to get her life back on track. Maybe she should pretend she had somebody new. She could create a fictional fling! His name would be, er . . . Richie. He would be a yachtsman. He'd be sailing around the world most of the time, but devotedly Skyping her on a daily basis – if indeed you can Skype from yachts. He'd sometimes send her a postcard from Papua New Guinea – she could easily forge one of those.

After some time hearing about Richie's adventures, Fred would get really fed up and he'd come back grovelling. Jess threw herself on to her bed and gave herself up to a wonderful fantasy. She'd be strolling through the park, ostentatiously rereading Richie's latest postcard and wearing the silk scarf he'd sent her from Brazil, when Fred would pop out from behind a tree and say, 'Jess, you goddess, I've got to apologise. I've behaved really badly, I'm so sorry. I adore you with every breath in my body – please forgive me!' And he'd throw himself down on his knees before her.

Jess was deep in this daydream when, dimly and far away, she heard the house phone ring. Then it stopped as Granny answered it. Moments later she called up the stairs, 'Jess! Phone call for you!'

Jess bounded off the bed. 'I'll take it in Mum's study!' she called back. She didn't want Granny eavesdropping – she had a feeling this phone call could be something really important. She flew into Mum's study and grabbed the phone. 'Hi!' she said, her heart pounding. 'This is Jess.'

She heard Granny put the other phone down in the kitchen. Suddenly the silence was a lot more private.

'Hi, Jess,' said a boy's husky voice. 'I've . . . I'm ringing to apologise, really. What I did wasn't so smart and it must have been seriously annoying. Can we talk? Could I meet you in the park in, say, ten minutes? By the bandstand?'

Jess was speechless. Though the voice was a boy's, it wasn't Fred's. Who was it? Dazzled and disorientated by the fact that this phone call was the very same conversation that she'd just been having in a fantasy about Fred, Jess couldn't think straight.

'Sorry,' she stammered. 'Uh, who is this?'

'Oh, sorry! It's Luke.'

184

Chapter 25

Jess dived back into her fleece and within minutes she was at the park gates. The sound of children's voices and distant music playing somewhere reminded her of the great times she and Fred had had here. Last summer, they'd spent every available moment under that cherry tree. All the trees were now bare and frosty. *A bit like my heart*, thought Jess grimly. *Not to mention my frozen toes.*

She couldn't help smiling wistfully as she remembered the ways Fred used to greet her – always funny and always different. One time she had approached him and he'd put on an expression of terror and hissed, 'No! I have no money! Go away or I'll call the police!'

Another time he'd pretended not to recognise her. 'Sorry?' he'd murmured. 'Have we met? Was it . . . at the circus? I can't remember your name, but your heads are familiar.'

Another time he . . . But there was the bandstand, and Luke was sitting – well, sort of lounging – on the balustrade and leaning against one of the carved posts. He looked elegant and casual, like a male model showing off a desirable jacket. And actually his jacket was rather smart – it looked like a genuine US vintage baseball number.

Fred would never have managed to sprawl so elegantly on the balustrade. He would have been standing there awkwardly, with his hands in the pockets of his scruffy anorak and a bit of hair sticking up in ridiculous tufts.

As Jess approached Luke, the wintry sun came out and Luke's curly fair hair was transformed into a kind of golden halo. *My goodness!* thought Jess. *I hope he's not supernatural or something. But if he is capable of miracles, I might ask him for a non-invasive overnight breast enhancement, in return for my immortal soul.*

'Hi!' said Jess. Luke leapt athletically off the balustrade and landed gracefully on his feet. If Fred had tried to do that he would have broken his leg in three places.

'Thanks so much for coming. How are you? Isn't it an amazing day?' he said, grinning.

Jess felt slightly surprised by his elaborate politeness

– he sounded like a grown-up. So far, her day had been unmitigated horse manure – apart from Granny's soup, of course. But she couldn't begin to explain that to Luke. The whole subject of Fred, Jodie and all that mess was off-limits.

They started to stroll around the park. Everywhere she looked Jess saw a place where, not so long ago, Fred had been kidding around.

'I just wanted, you know, to sort of apologise, in a way . . .' Luke was burbling on.

Jess found it hard to concentrate. She was remembering a time when some American tourists had asked what time the park closed, and Fred had pretended to be Russian.

'You know – for what I did last night . . .' Luke went on.

They were passing a fountain where Fred had once washed his hair – well, stuck his head under the arching spray. It had been a really, really hot day last summer. Emerging, dripping, Fred had said, 'I've always admired the way dogs shake themselves after they've got wet – I think I'll try it.' And he'd shaken his head violently from side to side until he'd made himself stagger, then he'd pretended his head had got stuck on one side and he'd come up to her with his face all kind of twisted, and said in thick, slurred speech, like something out of a horror movie, 'I think my brain's come off its stalk. Quick – call a doctor!'

'So . . .' Luke was still rabbiting on about something. He seemed to be feeling bad about the way he'd behaved at the party. OK, he'd bitten Jodie's neck without being introduced, but that was standard behaviour for vampires. He was still apologising. She really had to reassure him or this could get tedious.

'Stop apologising, Luke!' she urged him, banishing all memories of Fred for a split second. 'You have absolutely no reason to apologise.'

'You didn't mind what I did, then?'

'Everything's fine!'

'Really?' Luke was oddly lacking in confidence right now – it wasn't like him at all. 'It didn't seem, well, melodramatic or anything?'

'Luke, we were vampires! They're melodramatic – it's their style!'

'So you really don't mind?'

Jess laughed. 'Why should I?'

Luke beamed and suddenly caught her hand. 'Oh, that's amazing, that really is amazing!'

'Relax!' Jess squeezed his hand reassuringly, then

released it. 'There's absolutely nothing to worry about.'

'It was such a lame poem, though.' Luke shook his head in embarrassment.

What??!! A huge explosion took place in Jess's head. *The poem? Luke had written the poem! Luke had written it, not Fred! Disaster!* thought Jess. *He sent me a love poem – and I've been assuring him that everything is absolutely all right!*

She had to say something. In reality they were still strolling along a path in a sunny park somewhere in southern England. But in virtual reality – which is so much more real sometimes – Jess was being whirled around in a tornado of dread, confusion, dazzling sparks and choking smoke. It's quite hard to make normal conversation in such a state of mind, let alone tell somebody that their love poem, though stylish, was inappropriate and unwelcome.

'In the cold light of day . . .' faltered Jess '. . . everything looks kind of different, doesn't it?'

'Well, you don't look any different to me!' said Luke. 'Hey! The cafe's open! Let me get you a coffee!'

Jess accepted, even though it had been in this very cafe that she and Fred had once pretended to have a row, just for kicks, very quietly (to make it more realistic) but still audibly (to entertain the other

189

customers) about his supposed infidelity with a fictional belly dancer called Carmen O'Flaherty. 'I'm sorry!' Fred had hissed. 'But I was dazzled by her revolving navel! I hadn't seen anything whizz round so fast since my last visit to the launderette!'

'Shall we sit in the corner?' said Luke. 'I don't want you to be in the draught.' Though she was still trying to drag herself out of the sucking swamp of Fred-memories, Jess couldn't help feeling slightly, well, amused by Luke's courtesy. It was so odd to have somebody who wasn't actually a parent looking after you and fussing over you. 'What would you like?' he went on as they sat down. 'Coffee? A sandwich? A wrap?'

'Given the weather outside, I'd like a fur-lined wrap, please,' quipped Jess, making a huge effort to get into the spirit of things. 'Synthetic, of course!'

'Ha, ha, ha!' Luke laughed, almost too loudly, and then he looked at her with eyes that seemed to shine. 'You really are amazing. I've been telling Boris all about you. He can't wait to meet you.'

Who was Boris, again? Ah yes – the friend who was coming next weekend, apparently to make a film in which she was going to star. Jess was beginning to feel slightly anxious about all that.

'Wait till he sees you!' grinned Luke. 'You look terrific in that colour, by the way.' He reached across and touched her hair, moving a strand slightly off her face.

Jess was startled. Luke seemed to constantly take the initiative, and perform acts that were quite daring and unexpected. It made her feel on edge, but there was something faintly exciting about it. Whatever would he do next?

'You really do look a bit Italian,' he said, gazing – there was no other word for it – into Jess's rather embarrassed face.

'No way,' said Jess, trying to laugh it off.

'No, really,' insisted Luke. 'You could be Sophia Loren's daughter.'

At this moment the waitress arrived to take their order. As Jess buried her face in the menu, she thought of the time she and Fred had been to this cafe, sitting outside because it had been summer, and she'd told him it was their anniversary – they had anniversaries all the time and their seven-and-a-half-week anniversary had been particularly memorable. Anyway, they'd been sipping their lemonade, and she'd said, 'Come on, pay me a compliment for once in your life!' And Fred had looked at her long and hard, and said, 'Well, you have no visible bogies, which is an improvement on yesterday.'

'So.' Luke peeped over the top of Jess's menu. 'What can I tempt you with?'

Chapter 26

'It was such a great party last night,' said Luke as they tucked into a couple of chocolate chip muffins. 'Your friends are so cool. I was talking to your friend Flora at one stage.'

'Oh, Flo! She's beautiful, isn't she?' Jess, in an attempt to head him off slightly, wanted to suggest that Luke might find some of her friends more attractive than herself.

'Yes, I guess so, in a Hollywood sort of way, but blondes don't do it for me, I'm afraid.' He stared deeply into Jess's eyes. 'I'm kind of in love with darkness.'

'Shame about your own hair, then.' Jess tried to keep things light-hearted because, though she really liked Luke, he certainly was coming on a bit strong.

'Yes, I wish I had long hanks of black hair hanging

over a pale and ghostly face,' sighed Luke. 'Still, it's amazing what you can achieve with wigs and make-up.'

'Are you going to be in the film next weekend?' asked Jess. 'Or are you the director?'

'Boris is the director,' Luke explained, 'because basically he can't act to save his life and he's about a thousand times cleverer than me. I can't act, either, but I can pose and look tormented, and that's all we need.' There was something quite nice about his modesty.

'So what's the story again?' asked Jess, getting interested. After all, it was her first break in the movies.

'There's this guy – me, as it happens – and he's haunted by the ghost of a girl – that's you, obviously. The audience are going to realise that she's dead, and after a while they're going to start wondering if he killed her.'

'And did he?'

Luke frowned. 'I'm not sure. It could go either way. What do you think?'

'Oh, murder every time,' said Jess eagerly. 'It would have to be a stylish homicide, though – nothing ugly like strangling.'

'Ha, ha! A stylish homicide! I like it!' Luke had rather a nice laugh. 'You're so funny! So what would a stylish homicide be? Not many victims get to choose their method of execution.'

'Death by homework,' said Jess, suddenly remembering the mountain of it waiting for her at home. 'Or ironing.'

'Ha, ha, ha!' gasped Luke. 'Come on, do be serious. How would you like to die?'

A family at the next table had started to eavesdrop on their conversation. The mother, a thin woman wearing glasses, looked concerned and faintly disgusted.

'Well, it depends. Are there going to be flashbacks?' asked Jess.

'Flashbacks? Er, possibly. What do you think of flashbacks?'

'I'm fine about flashbacks, only . . . Er, haven't you written the screenplay yet, Luke?'

'No,' he said, grinning. 'I was thinking there could be a lot of improvisation, you know, but maybe you could help me with it, this week after school?'

Jess hesitated. It was a while since she and Fred had written anything together. For the past few weeks she'd been distracted by trying to organise Chaos, the Dinner Dance of the Century. Writing a short screenplay appealed to her immensely. And it would give her and Luke a project, which meant he would have to be thinking about scenes and dialogue and stuff. He wouldn't have time to write her poems and gaze into her eyes and tell her she was amazing and funny.

'Just an hour a day after school?' pleaded Luke. 'Can't I tempt you? Flora was telling me what a great writer you are.'

'I'm *so* not a great writer.' Jess shook her head and laughed. 'I can barely scrawl my name. Well, OK, but it'll have to be after homework as well as after school.'

'After death by homework, yes, of course,' agreed Luke. 'I'll have loads, too. I'm coming up to exams.'

'Don't mention the dreaded E-word!' Jess shuddered. 'I'm going to bomb, big time.'

'But it won't matter!' grinned Luke. 'Because by the summer you'll be a rising young actress on the indie film scene!'

Jess wasn't quite sure what the indie film scene was, but she quite liked the sound of it. 'So how's this movie going to be distributed?' she asked playfully. 'Will we open in Leicester Square? Will I get to wear my killer heels on the red carpet?'

Luke grinned and pursed his lips doubtfully. Jess noticed again that he had quite nice lips, pouty and curved, a bit like a painting of a smiley angel. 'I'm not sure about the red carpet,' he admitted. 'Though we might find a piece of coconut matting somewhere. Basically, Boris usually puts our stuff on YouTube and we've had thousands of hits. We've even got a company.'

Jess was impressed. 'What's it called?'

'May Contain Nuts.'

'Great name!' Jess nodded in approval.

'Yeah, maybe . . . though we had an email from a woman whose daughter is allergic to nuts. It's not funny as far as she's concerned – she almost died once. So we might have to change it.'

'Don't change it too often,' warned Jess. 'I've had trouble with that. Flora used to be in a band – it took us ages to decide on the name.'

'What was it?' asked Luke.

'Poisonous Trash.'

'Great! I love Poisonous Trash. Hey! That reminds me, I promised my dad I'd cook supper tonight. He's busy with some huge diagram thing he's got to do for school – an exam timetable or something.'

'So what's on the menu?' asked Jess, finishing her coffee with a slurp.

'Uh, butternut squash kind of stuffed with cheese and herbs and things, with a tomato sauce.'

'Hey! You're a really good cook, Luke!'

'No, no, I'm rubbish. I just use Jamie Oliver's

recipes – they work and they're kind of, you know, laddish. Even guys who drive fast cars and punch walls can cook them without losing face.'

'I love eating,' admitted Jess, 'but I hate cooking. I must try and get into it sometime.'

'I'll teach you,' Luke offered eagerly.

Jess hesitated. She already had enough projects stacked up with him, though it was hard to say so tactfully. 'Not right now, thanks,' she said awkwardly. 'I've got quite a busy schedule, what with your film and everything. Plus my dad's around at the moment and he's a great cook – in fact, he's giving me cooking lessons.' (She was hastily improvising here.) 'So he might get kind of jealous if I had some from you, too.'

'Oh fine, no problem,' Luke said with a smile. 'I'd hate to make your dad jealous – that would be a first. I made a girl's dad furious once, but that's another story.'

As they got up and put on their coats, Jess wondered how exactly Luke had made a girl's dad furious, and who the girl had been. She felt a strange little glimmer of annoyance that Luke had ever had anything to do with girls previously, even though she'd spent the last half hour trying to pull back from him.

'Who was the girl?' she asked as they stepped out into the cold air again.

'Oh, just . . . It's a long story. I'll tell you sometime.' Luke looked a bit thoughtful and, for the first time that day, slightly hesitant.

For a split second his thoughts were elsewhere, then abruptly he seemed to focus back on Jess and made a movement with his arm as if he was going to hold hands with her. Jess thrust her hands deep into her pockets and set off down the path. Luke followed.

'Flora told me,' he went on as they walked towards the gate, 'that you'd done a lot of writing projects with Fred. Do you think he'd like to get involved in our movie?'

Chapter 27

'No! Don't!' said Jess quickly. 'Fred is great, but his thing is comedy, and besides he's very unreliable.'

'OK,' Luke agreed.

Jess wondered if Flora had mentioned the Fred-Jess history when she'd been chatting to Luke, but he seemed totally unself-conscious when he mentioned Fred's name and now, mere moments later, he was laughing at some ducks on the lake.

'Hey! Maybe we could use the lake as a location!' he suggested. 'A foggy day . . . no, a foggy evening . . . you rise, dripping, from the water.'

'Whoa! No mention was made of icy waters!' protested Jess. 'It's not in my contract and it's just not going to happen.'

'Fair enough,' Luke agreed happily. He went on chatting about locations all the way home. The film seemed to be a big thing for him.

When they got home, Jess marched straight up her front path, preventing a prolonged goodbye, and promised to see Luke again after school tomorrow, homework permitting. She was intrigued by the screenplay idea, but she wasn't completely easy in Luke's company. It was such a shame she hadn't realised he'd written that poem. Because she'd been distracted and not concentrating when she'd assured Luke that everything he'd done was totally fine, it had sounded as if she liked him.

As soon as she was back in her bedroom she got the poem out and stared at it. Was it a love poem or just a joke? *You haunt my dreams* – well, that could just be a reference to vampire nightmares. But inviting a vampire to come to your pillow and take a big bite, then calling the vampire beautiful was rather a giveaway. And that line, *Being Jess-less for ever just isn't an option*, when she'd first read that, Jess had jumped to the joyful conclusion that this was Fred begging her to come back. It had seemed so obvious. She sighed deeply. The poem had a completely different meaning now she knew it was Luke who had written it.

When she'd thought it was Fred, she'd found the

poem witty and amusing – just romantic enough. Now she knew it was by Luke, it seemed awkward and needy, kind of presuming too much. She screwed it up into a ball and hurled it into her waste-paper basket.

Then she started feeling sorry for it, and Luke. It was a poem after all. There's something a little bit, well, sacred about poems. It wasn't Luke's fault. He was a lovely boy, really: polite, considerate, confident, funny – although in a different way from Fred. Kind, good-looking . . . It seemed cruel to throw his poem away. She picked it up and smoothed it out. She had to keep it – for a while, anyway. But she didn't have to look at it. She opened a drawer in her desk and shoved it away, out of sight.

Her phone pinged. A text! She grabbed the phone eagerly. Maybe *this* was the longed-for Fred Parsons Apology! But no, it was from Luke. Luke *again*.

WEIRD THAT YOU'RE JUST THE OTHER SIDE OF THE WALL! SHALL WE KNOCK THE WALL DOWN AND BE FLATMATES?

Jess sighed again. If only Fred would bombard her with texts, tell her she was amazing and looked Italian. If only Fred would send her love poems. But it seemed Fred wasn't about to do any of those things. She really had to root him out of her mind. Listlessly she tossed the phone on to her bed. It was time for history homework.

Next day, on the way to school, Jess vowed she would treat Fred perfectly calmly, as just another friend. She wouldn't be obsessed about whether Jodie was touching him or not. She wouldn't remember the wonderful times they'd had together. She wouldn't plan delightful ways to murder Jodie.

She was punishing herself, while Fred showed no signs whatsoever either of regretting being dumped or of regretting the behaviour which had led to his being dumped. If she didn't manage to make this new start, the only person who would suffer would be herself.

She would become her own life coach! She would train herself to not think of Fred, or she would think of him doing lame or disgusting things. She spent the next five minutes imagining Fred doing various disgusting things of a bathroom nature. Then she realised she was thinking about Fred again, even if it was negative, and thinking about him in the loo didn't make him seem as loathsome as she'd hoped. After all, he was human – everyone goes to the loo.

Jess spent some quality time imagining all sorts of

celebs going to the loo, and this was the most entertaining part of her journey by far.

As she arrived at school it started to rain, and she met Flora under the portico.

'Hey, babe!' cried Flora excitedly, grabbing her arm. 'Guess what? Jack's been selected to play squash for the county!'

Jess expressed surprise and delight, while secretly thinking that she'd been wrapped up in her own troubles so deeply it was almost a shock to be reminded that other people existed and that nice things could happen in their lives.

'Great!' She linked arms with Flora and they headed for the form room. 'We'll have to go to all his matches – dressed as cheerleaders!'

Flora giggled. It made Jess feel loads better just to be with Flo, thinking about her life for a change.

The form room was noisier than usual because Mackenzie was having an argument with Pete Collins about God. Or maybe he was having an argument with God about Pete Collins. Jess wasn't sure. Instantly she saw Jodie and Fred deep in conversation at the back of the room. Jodie was laughing and being vivacious, and Fred was listening and looking amused. He didn't have half an eye on the door to catch a glimpse of anybody who might have come in. No, no! He seemed totally oblivious to Jess, or anybody else for that matter.

'Let's sit at the front,' said Flora tactfully. She'd seen Fred and Jodie, too, and she knew it might hurt. She was such a great mate.

'Yeah,' agreed Jess, sitting down in a way that was kind of exaggeratedly relaxed. She tried to look as if nothing in the world was the matter.

'So . . .' said Flora, snuggling up in a pre-whispering kind of posture. 'Tell me all about –'

At this moment Jess was struck violently between the shoulder blades. It was Jodie, of course.

'Hey, Jess! Flora! Party at my place next Saturday, OK? We're going to have a bonfire and baked beans and stuff. A winter barbecue!'

'What's this in aid of, then?' asked Jess. 'Seems kind of last minute. It's not your birthday or anything, is it?'

'No, no!' cried Jodie. 'It's just a wonderful, spur-of-the-moment get-together because we had so much fun last Saturday at Pete's thing! I'm a mad impulsive creature and I must have fun!'

'Sorry,' said Flora quickly, 'but I'm going out with Jack on Saturday night.'

'Bring him to the party!' urged Jodie.

'No, we're going to the movies,' said Flora firmly. 'He's already got the tickets.'

'Fair enough,' admitted Jodie. 'What about you, Jess? You've gotta come! And bring that gorgeous heart-throb of yours, Luke! He can bite my neck any time!'

'No, I can't come, I'm sorry, Jodie,' Jess went on. 'I'll be filming all next weekend.'

'Filming? Ooooh!' cried Jodie, sensing an audience. 'Jess can't come to my party because she's *filming* all next weekend, folks!'

'Filming?' asked Jamie Greenstone, a boy with floppy red hair and a passion for movies. 'How come?'

'Who's it with?' demanded Jodie.

'Luke,' said Jess simply. She felt a bit awkward, talking about it like this. Jodie's wretched party was a nuisance. 'He and his friend Boris have made lots of movies.'

'Can I be in it?' demanded Jodie. 'Cancel the party! I'm gonna be in a movie!'

'No, I'm afraid you can't,' said Jess between clenched teeth. Though she herself had mixed feelings about the movie, it did at least give her the opportunity of firmly saying no to Jodie, which was a pleasant sensation even though it did fall short of the longed-for murder.

'Why not?' demanded Jodie. 'You must need extras!'

'We don't need extras,' Jess insisted. Most of the class was listening by now. If only Mr Fothergill would arrive!

'Who's in it, then?' asked Jodie.

'Just me and Luke.' Jess tried to make it matter-of-fact, but it did sound slightly romantic, and there were whoops and stupid catcalls all over the room.

'Is this, like, a lovey-dovey movie?' asked Mackenzie – the idiot.

Jess felt herself blushing furiously. 'No,' she said hastily. 'It's more of a thriller, actually. I play the part of a ghost.'

'I'd fall in love with a good-looking ghost, no problem,' said Mackenzie.

'Hey!' Pete interrupted Mackenzie. 'How come you believe in ghosts but you don't believe in God?'

At this point Mr Fothergill arrived – not exactly God, but the nearest thing available locally. The hubbub faded away and some kind of order was created – everywhere, that is, except in Jess's whirling brain. She knew it wasn't over, either. There would be further interrogation at lunchtime. And now Fred knew she was filming, all next weekend, with Luke. She hoped he was gutted and looked forward to seeing symptoms of his torment as soon as possible.

Chapter 28

'OK!' said Jodie at lunchtime. 'Me and Fred challenge you and Flo to a Scrabble game.'

As it was still raining, it seemed unavoidable. 'Might as well,' shrugged Jess. 'If you can face being wiped off the face of the earth.'

'Fat chance!' sneered Jodie. 'You know Fred is a genius!'

They sat down – Jess was opposite Flora because she was her partner. This was a relief. Though she'd promised herself she'd treat Fred the same as normal, it would have been difficult having him so much in her face. He was sitting on her right, so she didn't have to look at him if she didn't want to. They chose their letters and laid them out. Jess had A, A, A, I, U, O and H.

'Mine is a cry of pain,' she sighed.

'Mine's a town in Poland,' said Fred.

'Mine's a disease,' said Flora.

'Mine's brilliant!' beamed Jodie. 'I've got the Q and it's worth ten points. So there!'

'Yeah, but have you got a U?' sneered Jess.

'It'll come, it'll come,' Jodie sneered right back with a grin.

The game began. Jodie put down MEN, Flora put down TREAT, Fred put down a Y to make TREATY and then added his own word, ZLOTY.

'What's a ZLOTY?' demanded Jess indignantly.

'It's the currency in Poland,' said Fred. 'Or it used to be the currency before they went over to the euro.'

'How on earth do you know that?' asked Flora.

'I was reading an old thriller, set in the days of the cold war,' said Fred.

'You and your precious thrillers!' snapped Jess. She used to delight in Fred's cleverness. Now it seemed to be turned against her.

'Well done, partner!' Jodie reached across the table and gave Fred a high five. Their hands were touching again.

How annoying! Jess had vowed not to notice if they touched each other or not. It was only a high five, after all.

'So.' Jodie was keeping the score. 'We lead by . . . fifty-six. Great move, Freddio.'

Freddio? Did Jess really have to put up with this? Jodie inventing pet names for Fred, right under her nose? But then, what did pet names mean? Hadn't she invented pet names herself, in her time, for all the boys in the class? Wasn't it just being playful and affection-ate? And who wouldn't feel affectionate towards Fred?

'Sorry, Florio,' she said, turning to Flora. 'I have a real bum hand here.' It was true: her letters were really bad. But the worst thing was that she couldn't concen-trate. Her wretched brain was busy all the time with the Fred-Jodie scenario. All Jess could put down was a miserable piddling little OH.

'Oh!' cried Fred melodramatically. 'Oh, oh, oh!'

'Five,' said Jodie, with an evil grin, recording Jess's pitiful score.

Jess picked up another letter. It was another O. At this point there was nowhere to go except into a ridiculous fantasy world. In the fantasy they were playing Scrabble, but Fred was putting down signif-icant words, like somebody sending signals in a Jane Austen novel.

REGRET, he put down, and then gave her a long, sorrowful, tormented stare. SHAME came next. Then

AGONY. Then DESPAIR. Then FORGIVE. Then FOREVER. When Fred *really* looked at her, though, he seemed miles away from sorrow or torment. In fact, there was a gleam in his eye which suggested he was more in the mood to torment her than suffer himself.

'So, this film you're in next week,' he said towards the end of the game, when he and Jodie were leading by 130 points and couldn't possibly lose. 'What part are you playing, again?'

'The ghost of somebody's ex-girlfriend,' said Jess.

'Wow!' said Jodie. 'Typecasting!'

It was a terrible moment. There was a split-second pause of frozen embarrassment. Jodie wasn't really a cruel person – just thoughtless and challenging – but that remark was a stinker. Fred blushed slightly and bent over to fiddle with his shoelaces. Jess felt an explosion of rage sweep through her ribcage for a moment. She was the one who'd dumped Fred, for goodness' sake! And for good reasons.

'Right!' Jess felt her face go scarlet with embarrassment and fury, and she had to get out. 'As we've been blown away, I think we should concede defeat. I'm out of here.' She got up, picked up her fleece and bag, and walked out, trying to stroll slowly so it didn't look like a stupid aggravated flouncing kind of exit.

The cold air of the corridor soothed her flaming cheeks. Half a minute later Flora caught up with her.

'Can you believe that Jodie!' she seethed. 'What a thing to say! Are you OK, Jess?'

'Yes,' said Jess, tight-lipped. 'I'm fine. Being the ghost of somebody's ex-girlfriend suits me just fine.'

'Look,' said Flora. 'Sit down a minute.' They went into the locker room and found a bench. 'How are you really? I mean, this thing with Jodie –'

'I'm fine,' said Jess. 'Really, I'm totally fine about it. Is it a "thing", anyway?'

'I saw them holding hands,' whispered Flora, distraught. 'Harriet says she even saw them kissing.'

A spear ran through Jess's heart. 'Excellent,' she said. 'It's up to them.' She knew it sounded lame. There was a long silence, in which she managed not to cry and Flora failed to think of anything to say.

'This film, then . . .' Flora changed tack. 'That guy Luke . . . he's really, really nice.'

Jess shrugged.

'It was obvious he fancied you.'

'Maybe,' said Jess. 'Poor deluded fool. He says I look Italian.'

'I've always thought that!' said Flora.

'Hmmmm.' Jess could see where this conversation

was going. 'I don't want to get involved with Luke,' she said. 'He's a nice guy, but I'd be on the rebound. It wouldn't be fair to him. It wouldn't work.'

'You don't have to get involved with him *really*,' Flora explained excitedly. 'You could just kind of pretend to, and make Fred jealous.'

Jess sighed. 'I don't think Fred would give a flying fandango whether Luke and I were an item,' she said listlessly.

'He so would! He's obviously edgy about it, otherwise he wouldn't have mentioned the film. I've been watching his body language with Jodie and it's not comfortable at all. He's not happy with the situation, Jess. He wants to get back with you, I know it. Don't forget, it was you who dumped him. Maybe he's waiting for you to make the first move.'

'Why should I?' Jess snapped. 'The ball's in his court. It's not difficult! All he has to do is dump Jodie and send me a text or something. Or call me.'

'You know Fred,' said Flora hesitantly. 'He's not famous for his backbone.'

'Well, he should try and grow one!' Jess was fired up now. 'If he'd rather drift off and not be with me any more, and be bullied into being Jodie's boyfriend just because he hasn't got the guts to go for what he really wants, he doesn't deserve me anyway!'

'That's right!' Flora agreed doubtfully. 'But maybe Luke does deserve you. Maybe you haven't really given him a chance because you've been so obsessed with Fred. But really, Jess, I think he's amazing, and so do all the girls. He's so polite and good-looking! Really hot, but kind of gentlemanly, too! And confident and funny. If I wasn't with Jack I'd have a crack at him myself! Honestly, what are you waiting for?'

Chapter 29

For the rest of the afternoon Jess tried to ignore Fred in a way that might appear good-natured and relaxed because she didn't want him to think she was hurt. She wanted him to think she was completely fine about everything, that she couldn't care less, because that was the way he seemed to be behaving towards her. Let him have a taste of his own medicine. She just hoped it hurt him half as much as it hurt her.

Finally the bell went for the end of lessons, and the corridors filled with a heaving mass of kids. Flora had gone early – she had a dentist's appointment – so Jess was going to be walking home alone. She got distracted for a couple of minutes because she couldn't find her mobile in the bottom of her bag, then she found it (in the bottom of her bag), then she went to the loo, and by the time she emerged the crowds were clearing. She headed down the corridor for the main exit.

Now, she told herself, *I'm going to have a nice relaxing walk home, and I'm not going to think about Fred even once.*

There was a corner she had to negotiate before she got to the main lobby, and as she turned this corner, she ran slap-bang into Fred. He was alone.

'Oh!' she gasped. They had actually physically bumped into each other – the first time they'd touched for ages.

'Seems to be your favourite word,' said Fred, hesitating and kind of gangling about on the spot.

Jess's mind was a whirling blank. 'What?' she frowned.

'*Oh*,' said Fred. 'Your favourite word?' He grinned, but the grin was fake – it looked edgy and anxious.

'Oh!' Jess realised, and couldn't help smiling as she used the word again. 'Well . . .'

There was a pause, an enormous pause, as they seemed to hang over an immense gulf where anything could be said. They locked eyes and for a moment it was as if all the bad stuff had never happened. Jess opened her mouth, even though she wasn't sure what she was going to say. She was torn between the impulse to throw herself into Fred's arms and the desire to kick him in the teeth.

Then somebody came round the corner and the moment fractured like a car windscreen in a gravel storm.

'Oh well – *oh* again – goodbye!' Jess murmured and turned away.

Fred looked startled. 'Goodbye,' he replied.

As she headed off down the road, Jess's heart was racing. Why had they said goodbye like that? They never said goodbye. It was always 'Catch you later' or 'Cheers' or 'See you.' Why that ominous, formal, sombre kind of word: goodbye? It sounded symbolic, a kind of confirmation in a single word of what was happening to them. A drawing of a line under it all, as if to say: that's that, then.

Why hadn't he said, *'Forget goodbye – let's get back to hello'*, and swept her up in his arms? Why was he so useless at taking the initiative? When she'd been so stupid as to blurt out 'goodbye', why had he just repeated it, like a blasted parrot? Jess felt a couple of tears trickle down her face, but they were tears of rage because she was more exasperated than anything. The word *goodbye* rang on and on in her brain, like a telephone ringing in an empty house. She would never play Scrabble again. It gave words a terrible kind of power and significance.

Jess realised she'd walked the entire length of

Laburnum Drive without even noticing. She'd planned to walk all the way home without thinking of Fred, but already she'd walked down two whole streets and not even been aware of where she was, so vivid was the tiresome presence of Fred in her mind.

For the rest of the way home, she told herself sternly, *I am going to think about other things.* Food was obviously an attractive option. Jess was planning a monster sandwich when she got home. Mentally she rehearsed it now: she buttered the bread, then applied a thick layer of chocolate spread, then some mashed banana and lastly a sprinkle of chopped nuts. She imagined how glorious it would be to place the top slice on, gently press down and then carefully slice it in half. Then, in her fantasy, she raised the divine sandwich to her lips – and suddenly there was Fred's head, tiny but recognisably Fred, peering out of her sandwich like a maggot in an apple!

Jess groaned aloud. The sandwich fantasy had started promisingly, but she had failed at the last minute to exorcise Fred. He'd not only ruined her life – he'd ruined her sandwich.

Jess abandoned all thoughts of food and instead planned a safari. She knew Fred would never want to go on safari – he wasn't really the outdoor type. He also wasn't at his best with animals; if they were small, he sometimes trod on them by accident; if they were big, he was scared of them. He had a real phobia about horses. *Stop thinking about Fred*, she reminded herself sternly.

The safari, then . . . She was in a jeep jolting over the grasslands of Tanzania or somewhere. There was a place she'd heard of called something like Ngorongoro. If only place names were allowed, she'd love to put that down in a Scrabble game. But no! She mustn't think of Scrabble. Scrabble was forever tainted by its association with you-know-who.

Jolting over the grasslands, then, Jess raised her binoculars to her eyes. 'There's a lioness over there, just below that thorny tree!' whispered her guide, a muscular dreamboat called Andy. Jess peered through the binoculars and scanned the grasslands. She saw zebras, lions, marvellous birds, and then – oh no! There was Fred, actually mounted on an ostrich as if it was a horse, whirling round and round and shouting for help.

Jess jolted out of her daydream. It was so hard, being on your own. If only Flora wasn't at the dentist's, then they could have walked part of the way home together and Flora could have distracted her with news of Jack's sporting triumphs and her dad's latest mood swings. On her own, Jess was at the mercy of her foolish brain, which seemed to be stuck on a loop.

It was a relief to get home. At least there would be other people there. As she put her key into the front door, she was distracted by a faint last fantasy – that Fred had somehow got there before her and was waiting in the kitchen with Granny, a big smile on his face and a long apologetic speech ready.

But of course only Granny was there, though Jess could hear Mum talking on the phone upstairs.

'Guess who brought this!' Granny grinned at her, pointing to the kitchen table.

Jess threw her school bag in the corner and looked where she was pointing. There was a big envelope marked *Jess* and a single snowdrop in a tiny jam jar. Jess's heart gave a stupid lurch, but she sort of caught the lurch, like catching something that was dropping off a worktop before it hit the ground. Fred would never have given her a snowdrop.

'Luke, obviously,' said Jess, trying to sound calm and ordinary. She'd learned her lesson. She picked the snowdrop up and sniffed it. It smelt of nothing.

'I put it in water,' said Granny helpfully. 'I didn't want it to wither. He must have left it on our doorstep, rung the bell and then run back indoors. I heard their front door slam just as I was opening ours. The envelope was just there on the doorstep, with the snowdrop lying on top of it. Isn't it romantic!'

'Yes, yes, very romantic, Granny,' said Jess teasingly. 'I know you're bowled over by him, but don't you think the age gap is a little bit too big? I mean, he's a teenager!'

'Ha, ha!' laughed Granny. 'If I was a girl, I wouldn't hesitate for a minute.'

'Granny!' scolded Jess. 'Gross! Never say anything like that again!' She was feeling better already. 'Now,' she went on, 'to keep me going till supper, I'm going to have just a teensy little sandwich, so bring me a large white loaf and a tanker full of chocolate sauce.'

'Aren't you going to open the envelope?' asked Granny, still hovering over the subject of Luke as if she was a fly and he was a sugar bowl.

'All right, all right.' Jess smiled indulgently.

She opened the envelope and pulled out a couple of sheets of paper entitled *Filming Schedule*. They were nicely printed on good paper, not scrawled on the back of something else, as they would have been if – no! She stopped herself from completing that thought. They came with a little note attached with a paper clip (a bizarre and somehow slightly disturbing detail).

Hi, B.V. (Hope you don't mind if I call you that.) Here's the filming schedule for next weekend. I'm afraid it will take up most of the weekend, so clear your diary! I've factored in some homework time on Sunday evening. Come round tonight as soon as you've finished your homework/supper. Text me.
L x

'There you are, Granny! Since you're so fascinated and charmed by him, feast your eyes on that.' Jess thrust the papers into Granny's hand and set about making her sandwich.

Granny sat down at the kitchen table, put her glasses on and started to read.

Mum came downstairs. 'Dad's finally moved the last of his stuff over to his new place,' she said. 'And we thought we might go out to the pizza place to celebrate. What do you think?'

'Oh.' Jess hesitated. It really did seem to be her favourite word. 'I was going to do a bit of work on the film script with Luke this evening – I'd sort of promised him, but . . .' She wasn't really sure whether she wanted to be writing the script with Luke or not now.

'Oh, that's OK,' said Mum cheerfully. 'The supper won't take all evening – Dad's got loads of unpacking to do, and besides, Luke can come, too. He's such a lovely boy, isn't he?'

'Why does he call you B.V.?' asked Granny. 'Or is it private?' she added with a twinkle.

'Something to do with vampires, I expect,' sighed Jess. 'Boring Vampire, I think it was.'

'Oh yes?' said Granny roguishly. 'I don't think he finds *you* boring at all.'

Chapter 30

Jess was slightly nervous about seeing Luke again, but maybe it would be easier seeing him in the company of grown-ups. Or maybe it would be trickier – if the grown-ups started teasing and hinting about dating and stuff. She therefore had to put her foot down now.

'If we ask Luke to come with us for a pizza,' she said, 'which is fine with me, by the way, I want you to promise you won't treat him as if you're trying to marry us off or something. That would be unbelievably embarrassing.' Mum and Granny looked shocked at the very idea. 'It's bad enough when you tease me about him when he's not here,' Jess added sternly.

'Of course not, love. I'm sorry if we've been out of order,' said Granny, and she scrambled to her feet. 'I'd better go and get changed – I'll wear that red patterned blouse, so if I drop any pizza down myself, nobody will notice.'

Granny was terribly sweet, of course, and Jess adored her, but she did hope she wouldn't do any catastrophic spilling, drooling or choking. Jess hoped Luke wouldn't do anything unusual, either. There was something unpredictable about him which unnerved her.

'Why don't you just pop round next door and ask Luke if he wants to come?' Mum suggested, careful not to use a matchmaking tone of voice.

'OK.' Jess marched straight to the front door without even pausing to inspect her face in the hall mirror, though it almost physically hurt to walk past a mirror without even a fleeting glance – it was like some impossible ordeal out of a fairytale.

Suppressing her slight nervousness, she rang the Appletons' doorbell. She had to be bold. Luke answered it.

'Hi!' she said. He blushed. This was awkward, and it made her blush, too. Still, she had to soldier on. 'We're going out for a quick pizza,' she said, her stupid face burning. 'Just my parents and Gran and me – would you like to come?'

'Oh perfect, thanks, I'd love to,' said Luke eagerly.

'My dad's out this evening so I was just going to binge on popcorn.'

'OK.' Jess smiled, but it felt kind of deliberate, like putting on a piece of clothing to cover something up. She backed off down the path. 'So, why don't you come over in about twenty minutes?'

'Sure,' nodded Luke. 'Right. Er, did you get the filming schedule?'

'Oh!' Jess clapped her hand across her mouth. 'Sorry! Yes, of course – it looks fine. Thanks.'

There was a short pause while both of them thought about the snowdrop but didn't mention it.

'See you in five, then,' said Jess, turning to go. 'I mean, twenty.' She tripped over her feet. Luke was watching her with a fixed, fascinated look. 'These feet of mine!' She shrugged and pulled one of her comedy faces.

Luke laughed and looked enchanted. Why couldn't Fred be enchanted?

The pizza place wasn't very busy – it was Monday night, after all – but Jess's dad was in the mood to celebrate, so despite the place being half empty there was a festive atmosphere at their table.

'So . . .' Dad rubbed his hands together and grinned

when the orders had been placed and the drinks had been brought. 'May I propose a toast?'

Jess's blood ran cold for a split second. Not a toast to her and Luke! Please, please, no!

'To my new start,' said Dad. 'Sorry, that sounds so self-obsessed. Let's make that to new beginnings!'

'There's something exciting about new beginnings,' said Mum, sipping her white wine. Oh no! Surely Mum wasn't going to make a clumsy allusion to the need for a new start after Fred! But no. 'And in the spirit of the evening, I'm going to make something of a new start myself. I'm going to redecorate the sitting room.'

'Oh no!' Jess shuddered at this dire news. 'Everybody's painting . . .' Her voiced tailed off. She didn't want to think about Jodie's wretched makeover of Fred's bedroom.

'Are you and your father doing any redecorating, Luke?' asked Granny. 'People often do when they move into a new house.'

'Well,' Luke said with a smile, 'I'm thinking of painting my bedroom black, but Dad says it's just a phase I'm going through and he won't let me do it unless I promise to paint it white again once I've changed my mind. Plus I'd have to pay for all the paint. So I don't think I'll bother.'

'I should hope not!' Granny shook her head. 'Black, indeed!'

'I painted my room dark blue when I was at college,' said Dad. 'In fact, I was into wall art. Do you remember the Greek gods fresco I did, Madeleine?'

'Yes.' Mum shook her head and laughed. 'Although I've been trying to forget it for nearly twenty years.'

'It wasn't bad,' pleaded Dad. 'Although I admit Zeus did have a very big hairy bottom.'

'Dad, that was a major mistake!' scolded Jess. 'A Greek god would obviously have had it waxed.'

Everybody laughed and Jess began to feel a lot better than she had done for a while. She loved making people laugh. It was what she was about.

'So, how are you and your dad settling in, Luke?' Granny asked a few moments later.

She was so sweet, always making sure he was included in the conversation. You didn't really have to worry about Luke being included, though – he always seemed completely at ease with grown-ups, not like F— No! Jess hastily banished the thought of the person who was not at ease with grown-ups, and concentrated hard on what Luke was saying.

'We're settling in just fine, thanks,' said Luke. 'It's

really nice down here and everyone's so friendly. I was worried about my dad, how he'd adjust.'

'Worried about your dad?' asked Mum anxiously, as if poised to worry about him herself.

'Well, yes, moving from the old house. I mean, he'd lived there since my parents were married.'

There was a brief silence, in which Jess's family all wondered what had happened to Mrs Appleton.

'There must have been a lot of memories there for him, then,' suggested Granny thoughtfully, managing the situation quite well. 'I think your father mentioned that your mother's not with you any more?'

'No, my mum . . .' For a rare moment Luke seemed to struggle to find the right words. '. . . Er, she went her own way a couple of years ago.'

'Went her own way?' asked Granny softly.

'Er . . . yes. She, er, she met somebody and, uhhhh, my parents weren't really suited to each other,' Luke admitted ruefully.

'Nor are mine!' joked Jess, trying to lighten the mood. 'Just look at them!'

'But, er, you are sharing a pizza.' Luke looked around the table. 'It's friendly and . . . um, nice.'

'Is it not very friendly between your father and mother, then?' asked Granny, who seemed, by her age and experience, to be best qualified to ask impertinent questions.

'It's not that so much,' said Luke hesitantly. 'It's just that she's living in Tasmania now.'

'Where's that?' asked Jess.

'Australia,' said Luke. 'She's living with a guy there.'

'Is he Australian?' asked Mum, fascinated. 'How did they meet?'

'He was on holiday in England. She'd gone walking in the Lake District with her friend Alice. They met in some pub in the rain. I think she and Dad were drifting apart before that, though. Mum's very sporty and energetic and outdoorsy and Dad . . . well, he's a bit of a bookworm. They'd already started taking separate holidays and so, I suppose . . .' Luke shrugged. He looked sad but resigned – not emotional or anything, thank goodness. It would have cast a bit of a shadow over Dad's celebratory pizza if Luke had launched into loud, raucous sobbing.

'I suppose . . .' Mum hesitated tactfully. 'If she's a sporty sort of person, Australia must suit her very well.'

'Yes, there is that,' Luke agreed. 'She's always swimming and stuff.'

'What does her . . . new husband do?' asked Granny.

'They're not actually married,' said Luke awkwardly.

'And his job – well, it's a bit . . . He's a chick-sexer.'

'A what?' exclaimed Jess.

'Go on!' Luke turned to Jess with a smile. 'You can laugh if you like. He's a chick-sexer. He spends all day sexing chicks. The chicks hatch and he can tell just by looking at them what sex they are.'

There was a bit of nervous laughter around the table, but Mum was uneasy about seeming to make fun of what might be a really painful subject for Luke.

'She must miss you very much,' she said gently. 'I suppose you can talk on Skype regularly, and so on?'

'Yeah, we do now and then. But in a funny kind of way my mum's never been very maternal. She said to me once, "when you're grown up we'll be best friends, but I'm not much good at this mumsy lovey-dovey stuff." '

'Oh dear,' said Granny doubtfully. 'You poor boy! You've had a lot to cope with for one so young.'

'Oh, it's OK,' said Luke with a graceful shrug. 'I think it's made me a bit more, well, self-reliant or something. And it makes a great line for parties, you know – my mum ran off with a chick-sexer.'

Everybody laughed, but Jess couldn't help feeling that underneath the gag, Luke was hurting a lot more than he showed.

Chapter 31

After supper there wasn't a lot of the evening left, but Jess and Luke sat down at his kitchen table to rough out a few basic principles about the film.

'So, tell me . . .' she began. 'What's the film about?'

'Well, there isn't a story as such,' explained Luke. 'We've more . . . based it around a situation and a series of images.'

'And the situation is that there's this guy and he's haunted by the ghost of his ex-girlfriend?'

'That's it.'

'So did he kill her?'

'I don't know – what do you think?'

'Well, if he did kill her, that would give it more of a story,' said Jess. 'You could get flashbacks of the actual murder.'

'But he wouldn't have killed her deliberately,' Luke said with a frown.

'Why not? She might have been really irritating! She might have driven him round the bend.'

'Hmmm . . .' Luke pondered.

'Why don't you like the idea of him murdering her?' asked Jess cheekily. 'It's got so much potential. Hey, you could even take it towards comedy. Maybe he wants to kill her because she never stops talking. She talks and talks until his head is reeling, then he grabs the nearest object and blindly lashes out.'

'What object would that be?' asked Luke.

'Well, if it was an ordinary kitchen like this one, he could try and murder her with something harmless, like a tea towel.'

'Why not a knife or a rolling pin?'

'Because this would be comedy, right? It doesn't have to be comedy, but it's just the way my mind works – he grabs the tea towel and . . .'

'Strangles her with it?' Luke was trying to get into this scenario.

'No, that would be too logical. He thrashes her with it but it doesn't work, so he grabs the dustpan and brush and attacks her with that – trying to sweep her to death, obviously . . .'

Luke laughed.

'Then he'd try and kill her with a variety of useless things. I don't know . . . a bunch of bananas, the scales . . . Like cheese. Yes! He could open the fridge and try and kill her with stuff from there. Ice cubes. The remains of a shepherd's pie. Margarine.'

'Then what?' Luke was still laughing and seemed charmed by her big idea. She was thrilled with it herself.

'Well, he finally does manage to kill her with something totally inappropriate, like, uh, an oven glove or something. And then he's got to get rid of the body.'

'How would he do that?'

'Well, if you continue the kitchen theme . . . he could make dozens of girlfriend pies! He could start a business delivering pies to offices at lunchtime!'

'And then what?' asked Luke, still smiling.

'Then she haunts him, I suppose,' Jess concluded, exhausted.

Luke smiled at her and looked down at the table. She knew he was going to rubbish her idea.

'I love your idea, Jess,' he said, looking sheepish. 'But it's totally different from what Boris and I discussed. We want something, well, realistic.'

'Realistic? With a ghost as one of the main characters?'

'Yes, why not? A psychological thriller, if you like. He's so obsessed by his ex that he just can't stop thinking of her – he sees her everywhere.'

Suddenly Jess remembered the fantasy she'd had about the sandwich, with Fred's head looking out of it like a tiny maggot.

'Oh absolutely,' she said seriously. 'I know just what you mean.'

'We envisaged that it was a portrait, you know, of a state of mind. I don't think he killed her . . . I think he dumped her and then, you know, somehow she died in an accident or something. And of course he's tormented by regret.'

Jess's blood froze. What if Fred died in an accident? Instantly she could see the power of the idea.

'Oh wow!' she breathed. 'That's so much better than my stupid comedy thing.'

'No, no,' Luke insisted gently, 'just different. I'd love to do that kitchen murder movie sometime, too – it's more kind of Punch and Judy though, isn't it? I mean, our film is sort of moody and, well, I expect it's pretentious, trying to be tremendously brooding and powerful and failing dismally but, well, I would like to try it. The other thing is, of course, it's always much easier to do serious stuff than comedy.'

'Is it?' asked Jess. She'd mainly done comedy, so she couldn't really compare. 'But anyway,' she went on, 'how does it end?'

'I'm not sure how it ends,' said Luke, smiling. 'Maybe that's something we can discuss tomorrow night – if you're going to be around?'

'Of course!' Jess was genuinely eager to contribute. OK, Luke hadn't gone for her comedy idea, but he'd already agreed some ideas with Boris and if you've already started imagining things, you don't want your plans railroaded by a complete stranger. Especially one who wants to turn your beautiful enigmatic moody brooding movie into a pie fight.

Mr Appleton arrived home looking tired from his meeting. Jess got up. 'Well, that was great,' she said. 'Very interesting.'

It was handy having Mr Appleton there – it made the goodbye so much easier. There was no hesitating and wondering what to say, what to do – a peck on the cheek? A cheery wave? A collision with the doorpost?

'See you tomorrow, then, Luke. Bye, Mr Appleton!' was all she said.

'Oh please,' said Mr Appleton, 'do call me Quentin.'

Jess smiled graciously. The urge to laugh had to be

firmly strapped away out of sight until she was back home. 'Oh, bye, Quentin, then,' she said, nodding.

Dad was having a cup of cocoa with Mum and Granny when Jess burst in.

'Mission accomplished!' she grinned. 'Luke can come. Guess what? His dad's called Quentin.'

'There's nothing wrong with the name Quentin,' said Mum sternly. 'What about Quentin Blake? He was your favourite author when you were little.'

'Oh yes,' Jess remembered. 'I know it's OK for celebs and writers and stuff to be called Quentin – it's just that having one living next door is a bit weird.'

'It's not weird at all. Don't be silly,' said Mum rather sharply. Jess suddenly detected a strange atmosphere.

'What's wrong with you guys?' she asked uneasily. 'Has something happened?'

'There's been a dreadful earthquake in Latin America,' said Mum. 'Tens of thousands of people have been killed, they think.' Jess recoiled in horror. 'Don't switch the TV on,' warned Mum. 'The news will give you nightmares.'

Next day at school the atmosphere was strangely subdued. Some people were behaving quite normally, others were talking agitatedly about the awful scenes which had been on the TV news. Jodie burst in and, as usual, her first act was to make a loud public announcement.

'Fred and I are going to run a half-marathon,' she said. 'In aid of the earthquake victims.' Fred entered the room from behind her, looking at the floor and getting in a tangle with his bag.

'Fred, a half-marathon?' asked Mackenzie incredulously. 'It'll kill him.'

Fred glanced at Mackenzie and nodded with the ghost of a smile.

Jess was boiling. '*Fred and I are going to run a half-marathon?*' What, tied together, like a three-legged race? '*Fred and I.*' She tried not to feel a terrible attack of murderous rage. After all, they were only trying to help earthquake victims. But when she and Fred had been together, he would never have attempted to run a half-marathon. Jess was burning with jealousy.

'Why don't you put on a charity comedy show?' asked Mackenzie. 'That's more your style, surely.'

'This will be a comedy show, don't worry,' said Fred ominously.

'Why don't you do it tied together like people in a three-legged race?' asked Jess sarcastically. 'That would give us all a laugh.'

'Oh, Jess!' gasped Jodie. 'What a truly brilliant idea!'

So that was it. Jess herself had given Jodie an excuse to put her arm round Fred for the foreseeable future – and all in aid of charity.

Chapter 32

'No!' cried Fred firmly. 'I'm not going to do this tied to anybody! It'll be as much as I can do to crawl across the finishing line anyway, without having to drag somebody along after me.'

'*I'll* be the one dragging *you*!' Jodie assured him cheerfully.

But Fred shook his head. 'No!' he repeated. 'Find another victim!' Then he grinned – to make his remark a bit more friendly, maybe. Jess watched like a hawk, despite having her head turned in the other direction to apparently look at a very interesting wall.

'Hey, babe! Shall we do the half-marathon, too?' asked Flora. 'Although I'd never get my dad to sponsor me – he's introduced rationing in our house. We're only allowed one chocolate each a day. It's so unfair!'

'One choc a day would probably keep an earthquake

victim alive,' said Jodie. 'You should give up biscuits altogether and give the money to me. Sponsor me! Sponsor me! Or, even better, join us!'

'I'll decide later,' said Jess. It was annoying that her irritation with Fred and Jodie had even affected her attitude towards something as important as a humanitarian disaster like the earthquake. Instead of thinking how horrible the earthquake had been, she was thinking how horrible it would be to watch Fred and Jodie running the half-marathon together – Jodie fussing over him, making sure he had a bottle of water, that his shoes were tied up properly, stuff like that. Jess sighed.

'*Shall* we do the half-marathon, then, babe?' enquired Flora again.

'No,' said Jess. 'Let's do something else.'

At lunchtime the sun shone. It was a wintry kind of sunshine, but Jess and Flora decided to get some air. Out on the school field, there was an amazing sight. Two figures were jogging round the athletics track: out in front was Fred, in sports gear, his long thin legs pumping away awkwardly, his arms flailing; a short distance behind him was Jodie, puffing along like a hen whose chick has escaped. Being slightly overweight and knock-kneed, Jodie was not built for running.

'I see Jodie is chasing Fred – literally now,' said Flora with a smile. 'But he's managing to stay just out of reach.'

'He's such a tease,' said Jess. 'But seriously, I never thought I'd see such a sight: Fred voluntarily doing something sporty.'

'Apparently he's going to sell loads of his DVDs, too,' said Flora thoughtfully. 'In aid of the earthquake victims, you know.'

'Well, all I can say is, it's amazing what an influence Jodie's had on him,' commented Jess, trying to keep it light-hearted. 'He's quite a reformed character now my evil influence has been removed.'

'Oh, I don't think this is anything to do with Jodie,' said Flora hastily.

'Nothing to do with it? It was her idea, Flo!'

'Well, it may have seemed like it was her idea,' said Flora, 'but . . . maybe Fred's trying to impress some-one else . . . ?' She gave Jess a shy, sidelong glance.

Jess sighed and shook her head. 'You mean me, I suppose? I don't think so. Look, he doesn't have to bust a gut running a half-marathon to impress *me*. All he had to do was send me a text or an email with the word "sorry" in it. But evidently that was too much to hope for.' Jess sighed again. 'I'm over him now anyway. Totally. How could anyone be serious about a boy with legs like that? Breadsticks are more muscular! When you watch Jack playing squash, you must feel really pleased. You're probably thinking, "*Look at those biceps – they're mine, all mine!*" '

There was a funny kind of pause. Jess had expected Flora to laugh and look self-satisfied: Jack was, after all, the nearest thing to an Oscar-winning heart-throb available locally.

'As a matter of fact, I'm thinking of dumping Jack,' said Flora.

'What!' Jess was shocked.

'Yes.' Flora paused. They were standing under a tree; its boughs were bare, but there were buds hinting at the blossom that was going to burst out in a few weeks' time. Right now it was Flora's revelation that was bursting out. 'It may seem a bit harsh, but I'm getting a bit bored with him really,' she admitted. 'He's so predictable. He just . . . I always know what he's going to say. We're kind of in a rut, like an old married couple, almost.'

'But he's so nice *and* so good-looking – I mean, we're talking five-star looks here.'

'Hmmm . . . I know, and when you first meet

people that's what you notice, but are looks seriously that important?' Flora's eyes were travelling restlessly over the horizon. In fact, it wasn't the horizon Flora was staring at. It was Fred, tiny in the distance but still recognisably Fred, running his heart out rather like a broken umbrella might get blown along the street in a high wind. 'Jack is boring,' concluded Flora firmly, with just a tiny sliver of ice in the tinkling cocktail of her voice.

Jess was dumbstruck. Flora couldn't care much for Jack if she was considering dumping him so unexpectedly. Unless . . .

At this point Fred's legs had had enough and folded under him; they could see it all clearly even though it was way over on the other side of the field. Maybe he'd fallen over deliberately as a joke, but whatever had happened, Jodie now fell on top of him. Flora laughed.

'Fred's so funny!' she said, and her smile made her voice sound soft and musical.

'Well, Fred's predictable as well,' said Jess, slightly on edge. 'I knew he'd have to fall over at some stage. I could see it coming. He's such a show-off.'

'But he's a show-off in a lovely way, kind of sending himself up all the time,' said Flora admiringly.

'You should try organising something with him,'

commented Jess sourly. 'You'd soon get fed up of his Oh, I'm Useless Act. It's his way of escaping responsibility.'

'Well, he's training for the half-marathon now,' argued Flora gently, as they watched Jodie get up and pull Fred to his feet.

Holding hands again, thought Jess sadly. It was kind of funny that Jodie had fallen on Fred, though – it was her way of showing affection.

'Let's go in,' said Flora, shivering suddenly. 'I'm freezing.'

They linked arms and walked back. Jess was still turning over in her mind the surprising news that poor old Jack was going to be dumped. How could Flora contemplate it so calmly? Maybe she hadn't ever really been serious about him in the first place.

'I just want some excitement,' added Flora as they arrived at the form room.

Somehow, this seemed ominous.

Chapter 33

'I've been telling Boris about your kitchen murder idea,' said Luke, beaming eagerly. 'He thinks it's totally brilliant and we should do it not next weekend but the weekend after. Or the one after that. He might not be able to come down every weekend. I suppose we could go up to Manchester – would you like to go to Manchester for a weekend sometime?'

Jess was speechless. She hardly knew Luke, and here he was, inviting her away for weekends.

'Afflecks is amazing,' Luke went on. 'You'd love it. There's a flea market, jewellery stalls, posters, loads of clothes – gothic, indie, punk – and not a chav in sight.'

'Well . . .' Jess hesitated. It did sound brilliant, but her mind was in a whirl. 'This is all so sudden!' she quipped, striking a fluttery pose.

'Go for it!' urged Luke. 'We'll have the best time. We can stay at Boris's. His dad made a fortune in telecoms and they've got this massive posh house in Didsbury and his sister's got the whole attic floor as a kind of flat. She'd love you – she's got a guest room up there, so you could stay there and do girly stuff while Boris and I perfect our kick-boxing.'

'Kick-boxing is girly stuff, actually,' said Jess sharply.

'I know,' grinned Luke. 'I've been kicked quite often by girls. But do come! Boris's mum can ring your mum if you like and reassure her that it's not going to be a wild party with a lot of screaming.'

'Well, if it's not going to be a wild party with a lot of screaming,' said Jess, taking refuge in irony as usual, 'I'm just not interested.'

Luke cracked up. 'Honestly, Jess Jordan,' he said, 'you are one funny girl. Everybody's going to love you. Boris is going to fall madly in love with you.'

Jess looked modestly at the floor – they were in Luke's bedroom and were supposed to be discussing the film script.

'I hope not,' she murmured. 'It can get kind of messy.'

'Has anybody ever fallen madly in love with you?' asked Luke suddenly. Jess was startled. Luke was

247

constantly surprising her – if what Flora wanted was somebody who was unpredictable, she should look no further as Luke was certainly never dull. This direct question made her feel uneasy, though – and she was already feeling a bit on edge because of the invitation to go to Manchester for the weekend.

'I once saw a small dog in the street,' said Jess, 'who was obviously quite smitten with me.'

'Ha ha!' roared Luke. 'I bet he wished he was your dog. I bet everybody wishes that.'

'I don't have a dog.' Funnily enough, Jess was beginning to wish Luke was a bit more boring. This barrage of attention was kind of hard to deal with. 'And if I did, Mum would have to take it on walks. I'm very bad at looking after things.'

'But of course!' Luke beamed. 'You shouldn't be looking after things – you should be looked after yourself – by a team of adoring flunkies!'

Jess cringed slightly but smiled awkwardly. And yet this wasn't unpleasant – in a way it felt good to be showered with compliments. Nobody had ever treated her that way.

'Now listen,' said Luke. 'I'm going to be even more irritating now and take some photos of you, if you don't mind.'

'No, no!' protested Jess, covering her face.

'Yes, yes,' insisted Luke, getting out his camera. 'When I said "if you don't mind" I was lying. You don't have a choice, I'm afraid.'

He was already peering at her through the view-finder, adjusting various things and fiddling with the lamps in the room.

'It's such a shame there's no natural light,' he said, clicking away from different angles. 'Could you meet me in the park immediately after school tomorrow? It'll still be light for an hour or two, and I want to try out shots in some locations – by the lake and under the trees.'

'OK,' said Jess warily. There was the feeling, once again, of being rushed along, like a ride at the fair when you just have to let go and surrender yourself to being whirled round in mid-air or hurtled up and down on a switchback ride.

'Good! Lovely! Lovely! Don't smile . . . that's good. Lick your lips – they need to be a bit more shiny . . . That's wonderful.'

'Let me go and get my make-up,' protested Jess. 'I've got loads of lipgloss and stuff in there. Plus my eyes are horrendous today – they look like currants in a bun.'

249

'Rubbish!' cried Luke, approaching from another angle. 'Your eyes are amazing – their expression changes from moment to moment. And you've got that satirical look which you do all the time – it cracks me up. I was trying to describe it to Boris, but I couldn't put it into words . . . No make-up, please. You look great as you are, without any.' Little did he realise Jess had spent half an hour on her present 'natural' look.

'What about in the film?' she asked. 'I'll have to use loads of make-up then to make myself look dead.'

'Oh, yes, in the film, of course,' agreed Luke. 'But not now . . . Look towards that lamp for a minute and just relax your mouth. Now look back at me over your shoulder . . . Fantastic!'

Jess's initial awkwardness began to melt away. She was obviously going to have to put up with this, because Luke was very determined and in order to escape she'd have to make a bit of a scene, when he wasn't doing anything disrespectful, just taking a lot of photographs of her and commenting on how good she looked. Jess knew that some people in remote parts of the world don't like having their photo taken because they feel the photographer is stealing their soul, but she didn't feel like that at all

– in fact, she didn't quite understand what had made her think of it.

After a while, she relaxed into it and began to parody pin-up poses: Marlene Dietrich – all serious smoulderingness, then Marilyn Monroe – soft and daffy, then Lara Croft – challenging and hard.

'Stop, stop,' Luke said, laughing. 'This is supposed to be serious! Actually, I think I have enough now.' He lowered his camera and looked directly at her one more time, as if trying to spot a tiny aspect of her which he hadn't managed to capture.

'And I was just beginning to enjoy myself.' Jess sighed teasingly.

'Well, don't forget I want another session in the park tomorrow,' said Luke. 'In the meantime I'll mess about with these – I've got this amazing software that can do things with photos you'd never believe – so after it gets dark tomorrow we can come back here and I'll show you the final result. You'll look like a million dollars – although apparently the dollar's a bit dodgy nowadays, so maybe I should say you'll look like a billion yen!'

He smiled at her and his eyes kind of became fixed on hers, and something strange happened deep inside Jess's tummy. Oh no! She was beginning to fancy him.

Chapter 34

When Jess got back home there was an email from Flora waiting.

Hi, Jess! I just dumped Jack. He cried. It was awful. I felt so cruel. But it had to be done, it was soooo the right thing for me. He's gone now. He calmed down eventually but when I said, 'We can still be friends, can't we?', he said, 'No chance!' Thank goodness he's in the Sixth Form and I won't see much of him at school! Anyway, I'm free now! Freeeeeee! It feels fantastic. Call me or Skype me and you can have all the gory details!

Jess wasn't sure she wanted all the gory details. She'd had enough turmoil for one day. Besides, she was still slightly tingling from the look she'd exchanged with Luke. He seemed to be getting better looking the more she got to know him, and right from the start he'd been one of nature's beautiful creatures, with his long eyelashes and curly hair and pouty lips. At first, he hadn't appealed to her – possibly because she'd still been fixated on Fred.

Maybe fancying Luke was a sign that she was getting over Fred at last. Being exposed to The Jodie And Fred Show every day at school was kind of hard to take – Jess had had to grow some secret defences, like emotional armour, not to care about it, not to flare up and say stupid jealous things. And all the while Fred was ignoring her, more or less, letting himself be rail-roaded along by Jodie and literally almost inviting Jodie to fall on him . . . Wait! No! Jess was getting hot and angry again all of a sudden.

She had to stop thinking like this. She went back downstairs and got herself a hot chocolate. Mum was asleep in front of the TV news (more earthquake sadness) and Granny had gone to bed. Jess tiptoed upstairs again. She sat on her bed and stared at the wall. Beyond that wall was Luke, presumably working on the photos of her. She'd lost count of the compliments he'd paid her since they'd met. It had felt strange, being swept along by his enthusiasm while in some deep place in her heart was still preoccupied with Fred. But Luke's relentless campaign of adoration was beginning to have an effect.

She whizzed a brief reply to Flora saying she'd been out all evening and was tired and needed to sleep, but they could talk tomorrow. Then, as she sent it, an email from Luke popped up in her inbox. *Are you the other side of the wall right now? Wish I had X-ray eyes! You should see these photos – they're stunning!*

Yes, I am on the other side of the wall, Jess replied. *It's a bit unfair as you now have photos of me so you've stolen my soul, but I don't have a single one of you.*

It was a bit flirty maybe, but Jess was feeling a bit flirty. It was a relief to be flirty, to spend time with somebody who boosted her self-esteem. If she'd been organising a dinner dance with Luke instead of Fred it wouldn't have been a five-star fiasco. It would have been a 100 per cent triumph. She felt that Luke would go through fire for her. OK, he always came on a bit strong, but that was really nice and positive after Fred's half-hearted, cowardly attitude.

Another email landed in her inbox. *You don't need a pic of me to steal my soul because you've done that already.* Jess felt her cheeks burn as she read this and her stomach sort of turned over (but not in a gross way).

But if you want an image to stick pins in, I've attached one of me looking like a complete moron. It was nice, the way he softened the dramatic declaration with a little joke about the photo.

Jess opened the attachment and Luke jumped into view on her screen. He'd obviously taken the photo by staring directly into his laptop's integral camera, but it seemed as if he was staring straight into her eyes. His expression was serious. She admired his lips again. They were curved and pouty. What wouldn't *she* give for lips like that! She began to look forward to seeing him in the park after school tomorrow. She needed to make a comment on the photo, though.

Nice one! Ever thought of becoming a stage hypnotist? Keeping the tone light was still a priority.

Only if you'll be my assistant in silver high heels and an ostrich feather! The answer came whizzing back.

OK, it's a deal, Jess replied. *Now you must excuse me, I have to spend some quality time with Napoleon.* Her history chapter had to be read.

Lucky old Napoleon, came Luke's reply. And then there was silence. Jess waited, hesitating. She didn't want to say any more, because things had got just a tiny bit dangerous and instead of being freaked out by it, now she was enjoying it. She switched off her laptop and went to bed.

It was hard to concentrate on *Napoleon's Rise to Power* with her head reeling with distracting new feelings. She felt really good about life for the first time in ages. She stared at the same paragraph for twenty minutes while her brain replayed the events of the day over and over, some bits in slow motion, until she fell into a light doze.

Suddenly she was in a tiny plane, a really old-fashioned one, seated behind a pilot, and they were taxiing to take off in a small aerodrome somewhere. There was almost a feeling that they were back in the 1940s.

Who was the pilot? As they turned at the end of the runway to begin their take-off, the pilot reached back and squeezed her hand. She recognised Luke's long fingers and now she realised that it was his fair curls that were escaping in little spirals from the edge of his vintage flying helmet.

'Luke!' she called in panic. 'Have you had flying lessons?'

'Don't worry!' he replied above the noise of the engine. 'You'll be fine with me!'

Then the little plane accelerated down the runway

and lifted into the air. Higher and higher they went, up into the clouds, and Jess peeped down below and saw the countryside spread out before her, only it was like looking down at a map, because the roads and place names were literally printed out.

'I'm going to loop the loop!' yelled Luke.

'Oh no!' screamed Jess. 'Please don't!' Just then she kind of twitched and woke up. It was twenty past twelve. What an amazing dream! Kind of exhilarating, but terrifying, too. She must remember to tell Luke about it tomorrow.

They met by the bandstand again after school. This time Luke wasn't lounging on the balustrade; he was just standing there, holding his camera, looking impatient. As she walked up to him his face broke into an ecstatic grin.

'Great to see you! How was school?'

'Oh, just the usual torment,' said Jess lightly. It had been, too – she'd had to listen to Flora going on about her wonderful liberation from Jack, and she'd had to watch The Jodie And Fred Show, which today had revolved around cakes as Jodie had baked some chocolate brownies and brought them to school in a plastic box.

'This is to prove you can still lose weight if you get enough exercise,' she'd announced. 'Hands off, Mackenzie! These are for Fred and me! Two each! And we'll still lose weight cos we're going to go running at lunchtime and after school.' Then she'd offered the box to Fred, and he'd grabbed a brownie (one of his favourites, incidentally) and made a kind of comedy act of eating it in the most boastful way possible, to make everyone else jealous. When he'd finished, he'd licked the crumbs off his fingers, smiled at the assembled company and said, 'Grade-A cookies, people!'

Maddening. Jess shook herself free of those irritating memories and smiled up at Luke.

'How was your day at the office, dear?' she asked in a parody housewife voice.

'Oh, it revolved around showing off, as usual,' smiled Luke. 'But I had something awesome to show off today. Look!' He showed her his phone. There, looking moody and haughty and somehow mysteriously glamorous, was a photo of Jess herself.

'Oh no!' she cried. 'I look like such a poser!' It was far from true – she was charmed by the image of herself, but she couldn't say so.

'I've been boring everyone at school with it,' said

Luke. 'And I've gained a huge amount of cred as a result. Now I'm not just the nerdy new boy – I'm the nerdy new boy with a goddess on his phone.'

'Don't call me goddess, please!' quipped Jess, feeling flattered but embarrassed at the same time. 'I'm supposed to be travelling incognito!'

Luke laughed and got his camera out. 'OK . . .' He started to look around. 'How about a few moody shots under those trees, for a start? And no kidding around now – this is serious stuff. You're a tormented ghost, remember?'

'What's my motivation?' asked Jess, smiling, as they walked towards the lake.

'Your motivation? Ha, ha! You're determined to scare the living daylights out of me – that's your motivation. Stand there, against that tree trunk. Yes! Don't lean, though – hover.'

Jess tried her best to hover, but it can be a tricky undertaking when your Body Mass Index is almost 26.

'Great!' Luke looked down the viewfinder. 'Fantastic! Now look more sulky!' Jess turned up the sulk. 'Awesome!' said Luke, snapping away. Then he stopped and frowned. 'Stupid joggers in the background, ruining the atmosphere,' he grumbled. 'That's the trouble with the park, and it'll be a lot worse on Saturday, I suppose. I'll just wait till they've gone past.'

Jess turned and, to her horror, realised that the joggers bearing down on them were Fred and Jodie.

Chapter 35

'Hey!' said Luke, focusing on them with growing recognition. 'It's Fred and Josie.'

'Jodie,' corrected Jess, starting to feel slightly sick.

Jodie's face was bright red and Fred was pale and puffing.

'Hi, guys!' roared Jodie, plonking herself down on a handy bench. 'Phew! I need a break! Whoa, Fred! Take five!'

Fred flopped down on the bench beside her. 'Good evening,' he panted in a posh voice. 'Quite pleasant weather for the time of year.'

'Guys!' Luke gazed in admiration at them. 'What is this? How many laps have you done?'

'Three so far! We run round the park after school,' Jodie informed him, getting out her water bottle. 'At lunchtime we run round the school field.'

'It's true,' said Jess. 'I've seen them.'

'We're training, apparently. It's instead of having a life,' said Fred.

'Fred! Don't be so neggy!' scolded Jodie between gulps of water. 'You know this is for a good cause. We're doing a half-marathon for the earthquake appeal, you see. You've got to sponsor us, Luke!'

Jess managed not to be irritated by the way Jodie kept using the words *we* and *us* because they were the obvious ones to use, right? It didn't imply anything except that there were two of them running round the park. And even if it did, so what?

'Sure, I'll sponsor you,' said Luke. 'What a great thing to do!'

'We're gonna lose weight, too,' Jodie went on enthusiastically, slapping her thigh. 'I'm gonna shed this flab!'

Jess noticed that Jodie's thighs already looked a bit slimmer and more toned. She became alarmingly aware that her own bod was suffering from a shortage of exercise. 'Hmmm,' she remarked. 'Good for you. The only part of me that gets any exercise is my tongue.'

'What? Snogging?' roared Jodie, laughing.

'No, no!' spluttered Jess hastily, blushing. 'I meant, you know, gossiping.'

'And snogging, too, I bet!' grinned Jodie, waggling her eyebrows up and down and including Luke in the joke.

'No way!' Jess insisted, embarrassed, between clenched teeth. 'My snogging days are over.' She didn't want Fred to think that she and Luke were on kissing terms. OK, she knew that he and Jodie had kissed – probably. Although she could easily imagine the way that would have come about. If Jodie was determined to kiss you, it would be hard to avoid, like a rugby tackle.

And anyway, Jodie would be easy to kiss. Jess had to admit that Jodie was cuddly and the more she exercised, the better shape she seemed to be in. OK, she was loud and assertive, but a lot of guys liked that. Especially weedy nerds like Fred. She smiled to herself. It was liberating, thinking of Fred as a weedy nerd.

'Your snogging days are over?' queried Jodie, looking sceptical. 'I bet you get a snog within a week! I bet you five pounds!'

'Done!' Jess extended her hand. Jodie's grip was strong and sweaty.

'Wait!' Jodie clung on to Jess's hand in an imprisoning way. 'How am I going to know if you've snogged or not?'

'You have my word as an officer and a gentleman,'

said Jess. 'I'll tell you if anything so gross happens.' She desperately wanted to change the subject. The very idea of kissing was way too delicate in this particular foursome.

'So, Luke!' boomed Jodie. 'Win my bet for me – give the gal a kiss!'

'It won't count if it's forced on me,' said Jess warningly, still looking at Jodie.

'I wouldn't dream of forcing my attentions on anybody,' said Luke a bit edgily.

'But you're supposed to be a vampire!' Fred pointed out. 'Or are you that rare kind of vampire, the polite sort which asks permission first?'

They laughed, and Fred gulped some water from Jodie's bottle. *Now their saliva has mingled*, thought Jess. But it had probably mingled already anyway. They were well on the way to creating a spit baby.

She occupied herself by thinking how good-looking Luke was compared to Fred. Fred was sprawled on the park bench, his thin legs and gawky arms all anyhow, looking breakable and somehow self-conscious in his scruffy old running kit. Whereas Luke was standing in a relaxed pose, holding his camera, wearing his sheepskin pilot's jacket with the collar rather smartly turned up, his hair glowing in the breeze, his green eyes sparkling, a perpetual happy half-smile hovering over his lovely pouty lips.

'What are you doing anyway?' demanded Jodie. 'Taking photos of Jess?'

'Yes,' admitted Luke cheerfully. 'It's kind of prep work for the film we're going to make this weekend. I took some yesterday, too – get a load of this!'

Oh no! He got out his phone! He switched it on, then held it out for Jodie and Fred to admire the photo of Jess which Luke had somehow edited to look glamorous and alluring.

'Amazing!' commented Fred. 'She looks almost human.'

'Great photo!' said Jodie in awe. 'She looks like a film star! Will you take some of me one day?'

'Sure,' said Luke. 'Any time.'

'Hey! You must come to my party on Saturday!' Jodie was suddenly in the grip of a terrible idea. 'Bring your camera! You can do wonderful shots of us all and we can put them on my Facebook page! I'm useless at taking photos – they're always rubbish. I tried to take one of Fred a couple of days ago and it was totally blurred.'

'That's because I am blurred,' remarked Fred. 'You captured my essence.'

 265

'We can't come to your party, Jodie, I'm afraid,' Jess said hastily. 'Remember, I told you we're filming all next weekend?'

'Oh pants!' snapped Jodie. 'I forgot.'

'We won't be filming in the evening, Jess,' said Luke tentatively. 'Only in the daylight. It's an outdoor movie.'

'Come to the party, then!' cried Jodie in delight. 'You must come! It's a winter barbecue! Wear furs and woolly hats! We're gonna have a bonfire and my dad's got a big shed with kind of French doors that open and turn it into, like, a veranda thing. You've totally got to come now, Jess, cos you won't be filming – we've heard the truth from your glam co-star!'

Jess was trapped. The dreaded party couldn't be avoided. 'OK,' she said, 'but Luke's friend is coming down from Manchester, so he might want to do something else. Have you got anything planned, Luke?' She was hoping there might be a family dinner or something because she so didn't want to go to Jodie's party.

'No, nothing,' Luke assured her. 'Boris is a party animal. He'll be over your place like a shot. You'll love Boris – he's a character.'

'Great!' Jodie beamed. 'I can't wait to meet him! People from Manchester are so cool!'

'Apart from the football team,' said Fred in a dark aside. Jess wasn't sure what this meant, but she was determined not to let the conversation get sidelined into football.

'Boris is the brains behind our films,' Luke went on. 'He's much more creative than I am.'

'So what's this film about, then?' asked Fred.

'Oh, it's nothing much,' said Luke modestly. 'It's about this guy who's haunted by the ghost of his ex-girlfriend. He dumped her, then she died and now he's tormented by regret.'

'Tormented by regret!' exclaimed Fred. 'Now that's what I call a lifestyle.' Jess wondered if he meant anything by this or was just helping the conversation along.

'And is Jess playing the girlfriend?' asked Jodie.

'Yes.' Luke smiled at Jess in a way which was almost proud. 'She's perfect for it. She looks just right. We'll give her that dead look with some pale make-up and smoky eyes.'

'That dead look is so *now*,' quipped Fred. 'I'm quite tempted by it myself. I might get into the Mr Dead thing once I'm through with being blurred.'

'So is this going to be on YouTube?' asked Jodie.

Luke nodded.

'Great!' she grinned. 'Should be a real laugh! Jess as a zombie! I can't wait to see it!'

'I'm not going to be a zombie,' said Jess snootily. 'Just a rather stylish ghost. Zombies are the chavs of the spirit realm. I wouldn't be seen dead as a zombie.'

Luke and Jodie laughed.

'You're a comic genius, Jess!' said Luke. He had a lovely laugh, kind of manly and musical. Fred's laugh was more a silent shaking, like a dog having a fit, although he wasn't laughing much right now. 'Jess has had an amazing idea for our next film,' Luke went on excitedly. 'It's going to be a comedy murder in a kitchen. It's hilarious, and we're probably going up to Manchester to film it. Yessss!' Suddenly he flung his arm round Jess's shoulders. 'You could be looking at the next big comedy partnership!'

Jess cringed outwardly and inwardly – it was the biggest cringe since cringing had become an Olympic event. She couldn't look at Fred because she felt as if she was a dartboard waiting to be pierced. The Next Big Comedy Partnership, of course, had always been her and Fred.

'What are you going to be called?' asked Jodie. Thank goodness she hadn't mentioned anything about Jess and Fred's history. Maybe she was showing a bit of tact for once – or perhaps it just hadn't dawned on her that Luke had stumbled into such a dodgy area.

'I dunno . . .' Luke frowned, puzzled.

'So,' pondered Jodie. 'You could be Jordan and – what's your surname, Luke?'

'Appleton,' said Luke.

'Jordan and Appleton,' commented Fred drily. 'Sounds like a brand of muesli.'

'It's no good,' admitted Luke. 'Terrible. And I think the word Apple is already somebody's intellectual property.'

'Jordan and Appleton, hmmm.' Fred hesitated.

Jess braced herself for some sarcastic aside and fixed her eyes on Jodie to avoid looking at Fred. It was her best chance of managing to stay smiling, though her smile was starting to feel twitchy, like a stalled download. Luke's arm was still around her, and she couldn't wriggle out of it without seeming rude or weird.

'There's bound to be some anagrams there,' Fred went on thoughtfully.

'Oooh, yes, do us an anagram, Fred!' demanded Jodie, as if ordering her dog to do tricks. 'He's brilliant at words 'n' stuff – we're gonna be Scrabble champions at school!'

'There's definitely Japan in there,' said Fred. 'And Lord.'

'Lords of Japan!' said Luke. 'Brilliant! Brilliant! You can be our PR team!'

Chapter 36

Boris turned out to be chubby and extremely chilled out. His hair was cut really short as if he'd shaved his head a month ago and was growing it back. His eyes were small and slightly slanted, and his mouth was big and smiley.

'This,' said Luke proudly, 'is the famous Jess.'

Boris nodded in a calm and carefree manner. He didn't mind whether she was the famous Jess or not, and would have greeted her in the same way if she had been a little-known piglet.

'This,' he told Jess, 'is the cinematic genius Mr Boris Padgett.'

'Take no notice,' drawled Boris, giving Jess a lazy smile. 'Luke is completely deluded.'

They were in the kitchen at Luke's house, and it was Saturday morning.

'Have I done the make-up right?' asked Jess. 'We've been talking about making it more realistic, you know, so I didn't overdo the ghastly pale face and graveyard eyes.'

'You're perfect – no, *absolutely* perfect!' Luke assured her. 'Do you think Jess looks dead enough, Boris?'

'Yeah, just right.' Boris yawned and stretched. It seemed the deadness of Jess was a matter of no importance whatsoever. Jess liked his chilled-out attitude. It made a nice contrast with Luke's energy.

'Jess and I thought it would be good to have a kind of flashback halfway through,' explained Luke. 'So we have the first few shots of him in the cafe and in the park and stuff, and he keeps seeing her, but then suddenly she's not there any more. Then halfway through we get a flashback to him dumping her, and then she throws herself under the train . . .'

'I'm going to need a general anaesthetic for that bit,' smiled Jess.

'Oh, it'll be fine,' Luke said. 'We'll just do some footage of you looking desperate on the train platform, then we can have you suddenly not there any more and a family standing nearby, looking round in horror and anguish.'

'Who's going to do the horror and anguish?' asked Jess.

'Boris's family can do that,' explained Luke.

'They've already done it,' said Boris, picking idly at a crust – all that remained of the boys' massive breakfast. 'We did the horror and anguish last Thursday when we went to meet my dad off the train. It's in the can.' He patted the camera lying on the table.

'But won't it be a different location?' Jess was worried about continuity.

'No, it'll be cool,' Boris assured her.

'It might be deliberately vague,' explained Luke. 'In a postmodern kind of way. Railway stations, they're all the same: Manchester Piccadilly, Grand Central Station . . .'

'Oh!' Jess relaxed. It wasn't her movie after all, even though she had a starring role. In the past, when she'd written sketches to perform with Fred, it had been her responsibility to get things right; now all she had to do was enjoy herself.

Luke got up. 'So! Shall we go?'

Just at this moment his dad came downstairs. 'Luke, I need your advice for a sec,' he said, with his usual sweet, sad smile. 'I'm wrestling with this computer program and unless I get some help I'm going to go mad by eleven thirty.'

'Sure,' said Luke. 'Won't be a mo.' He followed his dad upstairs to his den.

There was a strange, slightly awkward pause. Jess had already formed the impression that Boris was a guy who couldn't be bothered to do a lot of things, and the prospect of having to talk to him on her own made her feel ever so slightly nervous, in case he couldn't be bothered to talk to her. There was never any problem like that with Luke – she'd never met anyone so easy to talk to – so when he went out of the room it left a huge uncomfortable gap.

'Don't worry about anything,' Boris said, rubbing his head in a dozy way. 'Everything's cool and we're gonna have a ball.' He pulled a laptop across the table and flipped it open. 'Look at this video,' he smiled, getting into the YouTube website. 'It's hilarious.'

'Is this one of yours?' asked Jess.

'Nah. It's these saddos who spend all day filming their dogs. There's this one of a dog skateboarding and one of a Jack Russell terrier surfing. He's got a life jacket on and everything.'

They laughed at the dog videos, and it was all right – Jess didn't have to make conversation. Everything was definitely easy-going with Boris.

'I bet you miss Luke,' she said, while Boris did a

search on 'dog skiing'. 'Since he moved down here, I mean.'

'Yeah, he's a bit of an old legend up in Manchester,' said Boris. 'I suppose you know he won that photographic prize?'

'No?' Jess was intrigued. 'He never mentioned it.'

'No, well, he wouldn't. It was awarded for photos he'd taken while he was teaching in Namibia last summer . . . He's told you he's been to Namibia, right?'

'No!' Jess was amazed. 'I suppose we haven't known each other that long . . . but he's done some teaching already?'

'Yeah, they do these summer programmes – you know, teaching English and computer skills – and, uh, he was also involved in an Aids orphans project. I think that's where he took the photos.'

'I thought only college students did that kind of thing,' said Jess.

'You know Luke's eighteen, right?'

'No, I didn't know that. I seem to know nothing about him!'

'Well, he missed a lot of school in the Lower Sixth because of a car crash – he had to have two ops on his knee and he just decided to start over so he's a year older than the rest of us.'

'So he went to Namibia even though he had a dodgy knee?'

Boris shrugged. 'He is a bit of a boring British hero. He hasn't rescued a maiden from a dragon yet, but give him time. You could be that dragon. Oh, sorry, I mean that maiden.' Jess laughed. Then they heard Luke at the top of the stairs. 'Get a load of this,' Boris said, returning to YouTube. 'This is people who've taught their dogs to say "I love you" – allegedly.' They settled down to watch the video. 'Don't mention any of that other stuff,' murmured Boris as Luke clattered downstairs. 'It embarrasses him.'

'Sorry about that,' said Luke, smiling. 'My dad is such a dinosaur when it comes to computers.' He smiled at Jess, and she felt a strange new kind of excitement to be admired by this boy who had been through so much and done so many amazing things.

Suddenly she didn't mind the thought of going to Jodie's party. In fact, she was looking forward to it. It was as if some last tiny little shred of anxiety about seeing Fred had shrivelled away and been replaced by the marvellous thought that she was going to be in the company of such a great guy as Luke. The more she found out about him, the more in awe of him she was – and the more surprised that he seemed to like her so much. *'You've already stolen my soul.'* Wow! Nobody had ever said that kind of thing to her before, but now she hoped it would be the first of many wonderful compliments.

Chapter 37

Although it was Jodie's party, it was Flora who met them in the hall. She was dressed in black trousers and a scarlet jumper that Jess had never seen before. She looked stunning. Of course, she was celebrating her 'liberation' from Jack. Jess had an uneasy, ominous feeling which she couldn't quite identify.

'Wow!' gasped Jess. 'Have you had a makeover or what, Flo?! Blondes in red – such a classic combo!'

'Aren't you going to introduce me?' asked Flora, casting a coy glance at Boris. Jess did the honours, and left them talking in the hall while she and Luke went through to the garden.

Jodie had made it look really nice – there were tea lights burning everywhere and, as promised, a bonfire and a barbecue. Jodie's dad's shed was open and inside were a couple of old sofas covered with blankets and rugs, where everyone was sitting chatting.

'Hi, Luke! Hi, Jess!' Jodie beamed and gave Jess a hug. 'You're looking amazing! How did the filming go?'

Jess realised that she felt quite fond of Jodie sometimes. She'd certainly set up a wonderful party. 'The filming went great, thanks,' she said.

'What's Boris like? Where is he? Did he come?' asked Jodie.

'He's been captured by Flora,' explained Luke, with a smile. 'They're in the hall.'

'But what's he like?' repeated Jodie impatiently. 'I remember Luke telling us he was the world's next great film director.'

'He's brilliant,' Jess told her. 'I mean, he's very laid-back, but he takes his time to get shots right and he has these moments of real inspiration. We were filming this afternoon in the park, and I was supposed to suddenly appear on the bandstand and stare at Luke and freak him out, and Boris said, "Not so much like a dog – more like a cat." I'd been gazing at Luke kind of like a Labrador wanting to go for a walk. Once I started thinking of myself as a cat, it worked much better apparently.'

'Cats are aloof,' said Luke. 'They just couldn't care less, could they?'

'No,' agreed Jess. 'And I've decided to be a cat all the time from now on.'

'Yeah, right.' Jodie looked preoccupied. 'Where's Fred? He was here just now.'

Jess realised with surprise that she hadn't even thought about Fred for hours and hours. Flora wasn't the only one enjoying a liberation.

'Your dad's shed looks lovely,' said Jess.

'Mmmm,' replied Jodie, still looking around. 'It kind of doubles as a summer house . . .'

'Or winter house!' said Luke. 'I've brought my camera, Jodie, so shall I start taking some photos now?'

'Oooh, yes, please! Ah, here comes Fred! Where have you been?' She sounded angsty.

'I've discovered that there's this thing called a toilet,' Fred said sardonically. 'I think it's going to make a big difference to my life. You should try it one day,' he added to Luke.

Luke chuckled. 'How's the training going?'

'Well –' Fred began.

'Not now, Fred!' Jodie interrupted. 'I asked you to bring out the tray of jacket spuds, remember?'

'Oh, sorry.' Fred shrugged. 'I was distracted by an interesting book in the loo.'

'Fred! You said you'd help! I'm trying to organise

food for people here, you dummy!' Jodie nagged good-naturedly.

'What can I do to help?' asked Luke, immediately putting away his camera. 'Tell me what you need, Jodie, and I'll do it.'

'Oh, thanks, Luke!' Jodie beamed at him. 'Come to the kitchen with me.' She led him off.

Jess and Fred were on their own together for a moment, the firelight flickering on their faces.

'That guy seems to walk on water,' said Fred, with a rueful half-smile.

'You don't know the half of it!' Jess couldn't resist launching into a song of praise about Luke, even though it felt peculiarly like boasting. 'He broke his leg in the Lower Sixth –'

'Broke his leg? Wow! Why didn't I think of that?'

'Shut up, Fred. Listen. He broke his leg and he had to have two operations, and then he had to start over again in the Lower Sixth, so he's eighteen now.'

'Eighteen!' Fred raised his eyebrows in mock admiration. 'How does he do it?'

'No, listen! As soon as his leg was better he went off to teach in Namibia, and he took these photos while he was volunteering on an Aids orphans project, and when he came back he won a prize for them.'

'The guy's a star. It's sickening. Wimps like me don't deserve to lick his boots. Could you get me a hair from his head? I could try and clone a Luke to live next door to me instead of old Mrs Macarthy and her smelly poodle.'

'Fred, stop being so silly. How's the training going, anyway? I'm really impressed.'

'Are you?' Fred gave her a sudden, strange, darting look. '*Are* you? Well, I've almost sort of impressed myself, to be honest. I always used to hate exercise, but it's really weird . . . while you're running your mind goes into a kind of trance – the nearest I'll get to a trance without medication, anyway – and you think about your life and stuff.'

Fred looked different: serious and focused in a way Jess had never seen before. And she hadn't ever heard him talk quite like this, either.

'I hate the way I used to be,' Fred went on quietly, looking into the flames. 'Useless, cowardly, spineless and sort of complacent.' Jess was quite shocked to hear him talk like this. 'It was all a mistake, my past life – a total disaster.'

Jess felt a spear of terror and her heart started to

pound. Did Fred mean that all the time he'd spent with her was a disaster? She hesitated, racked with strange qualms.

'So you're reinventing yourself?' she asked, trying to sound casual.

'Yes. You won't recognise the new me.' Fred gave her a quizzical look. 'I'm getting a nose job, too, obviously.' That was the old Fred back again, rescuing them from awkwardness with a joke.

'Jacket spud, anyone?' Luke arrived with a tray of baked potatoes. They smelt divine.

'Those were the spuds I was supposed to bring out,' said Fred, staring dolefully at them. 'You've stolen my spuds, man!'

There was a curious undertone to the situation, as if Fred was speaking in code. But Luke, offering spuds to everyone standing nearby, didn't seem to have heard him. They started to eat the spuds, using their fingers and scattering grated cheese everywhere.

When Luke had finished distributing them, he got his camera out again. 'Jess and Fred eating spuds by firelight,' he said, pointing his lens at them.

Jess felt uncomfortable. She had got used to Luke photographing her, but she somehow didn't want him to take a picture of her and Fred.

'Stand a bit closer together,' said Luke.

They shuffled closer, like two people who hardly knew each other. Jess felt the faint warmth of Fred's arm against hers. Fred was pulling faces and striking poses, as usual when there was a camera about. She wondered if that, too, would change once he reinvented himself.

'Would you mind, Fred,' said Luke once he'd taken half a dozen of them, 'getting one of me and Jess together?'

No! thought Jess. *That's what couples say on holiday, to complete strangers!*

'Sure,' said Fred, wiping his hands on his trousers. 'Which button do I press? I'm a bit Stone Age when it comes to cameras.'

He didn't seem to mind being asked – he seemed perfectly relaxed. It was so hard to tell what he was feeling.

Luke showed him how to work the camera and then came back to Jess's side. He put his arm round her and squeezed her close to him. Jess felt anguish and a sudden emptiness.

'Smile, please,' said Fred.

Chapter 38

Jess and Luke walked home together. Flora and Boris had wandered off into the night, hand in hand.

'What a brilliant party that was,' said Luke. 'I like Jodie. She's got the Life Force.'

'Oh, that's what it is,' said Jess, with a wry smile. 'I thought she was just pushy.'

'Well, if you've got the Life Force you have to be pushy, I'm afraid,' said Luke.

'I do like her a lot,' said Jess, surprising herself.

'Mmmmm, I feel really mellow now,' Luke said, sighing contentedly. They were walking down an avenue which Jess and Fred had walked down a hundred times. 'Look, you can see the moon peeping at us behind the clouds.'

Jess looked up. Clouds were scudding fast across the sky; stars twinkled one moment, and were extinguished the next.

Jess didn't feel mellow. The party had unsettled her. She'd been so confident beforehand, having had such a great time filming with Luke and Boris and hardly thinking about Fred all day. If only he'd been his normal self at the party, kidding around and throwing insults at her, she could have coped just fine.

In fact, she'd been looking forward to being there with Luke, almost as an item. Fred had seen them together several times now, and he and Jodie had obviously been together again, too. All the signs indicated that Jess and Fred were going their separate ways – and in a civilised way, as friends, without too much heartache.

Jess had started to fancy Luke, and she'd enjoyed that. The little frissons when their eyes met – that was delicious. But what Fred had said at the party – about his past life being a disaster – had hurt and disturbed her. And she hadn't even had the chance to ask him what he meant because a party isn't exactly the place to get into deep personal stuff.

'Come here a minute.' Luke caught her hand. The avenue was deserted. 'Jess by starlight,' he said. 'I should take a photo of you like this really, but it would spoil the moment. The stupid camera gets in the way sometimes – of real life.' He looked down at her tenderly.

He's going to kiss me now, thought Jess. She'd thought about it a dozen times, admiring Luke's pouty lips. His eyes grew large in the moonlight. Above their heads, a street lamp buzzed. Far away, an owl hooted.

Luke kissed her. *Here goes, then*, thought Jess. She gave herself up to it. The kiss went on for a reasonable amount of time. It wasn't too disappointingly short or too suffocatingly long. He tasted nice. He smelt nice. He was gentle. There was really nothing at all wrong with the kiss. It was just, well, empty. It was like buying a cheeseburger and then finding there was no cheese in it. Jess's heart sank. She'd been half looking forward to this moment, but it was clear it wasn't going to work. He seemed to adore her and she hated the thought of hurting him. However was she going to tell him?

They broke apart slightly. The street lamp above their head was buzzing like a demented mosquito. Luke looked down into her face, but the expression in his eyes was strange. Jess was half-expecting another kiss or a tighter hug, but instead he loosened his grip until he was just holding one of her hands, and in a loose, ceremonious way, like somebody in a Jane Austen novel.

'Oh dear.' He sighed. 'I'm afraid I've been very unfair to you, Jess.'

What? Jess couldn't believe her ears. 'How?' she whispered.

'I've been . . . behaving stupidly. I'm so sorry. I'm really, really sorry, Jess.'

'What are you apologising for?' Jess was puzzled.

'Ever since we met . . . ever since I first saw you . . .' Oh no. Not more declarations! 'You've reminded me of somebody.'

'Who?' Jess's heart missed a beat.

'There was a girl . . . in Manchester . . . Sophie. We went out together for a year. But when . . . when I had to move down here, I finished with her. I thought it would be too hard, you know, to go on seeing somebody when they're two hundred miles away and we're both still at school. I thought we could adjust to it and stay friends and stuff. But I can't get her out of my mind.'

Relief flooded through Jess. 'It's OK,' she said.

'No, no, I've been terrible. I've been trying, well, to forget her, by throwing myself at you. You do remind me of her slightly. She's dark like you. But the thing is, I'm still . . .'

'Still crazy about her?'

'Yes. I'm so sorry, Jess. I've been totally out of order. It's not that . . . I do like you. Well, I adore you – who wouldn't? – but . . .'

'We're never going to be an item?' smiled Jess.

Luke shook his head and bit his lip. He looked down at her. 'Lovely, lovely Jess! Can you ever forgive me?'

'There's nothing to forgive!' beamed Jess. 'I've been doing just the same thing!'

'What?' Luke looked astonished.

'Yes, just the same. I finished with somebody just before I met you, and I've really enjoyed our time together and I've been trying to, well, move on, but I've realised I'm not over him yet.'

'Hey! Amazing coincidence! Who is he?'

'It's Fred.'

Luke just gawped for a few seconds. 'Fred?' he stuttered. 'Fred? Oh no! The things I said – and the things I did! Asking him to take a photo of us together! I'm so, *so* sorry!'

'No, no, it's fine,' Jess assured him. 'That stuff was all cool. Getting to know you and Boris has been really good for me, and the film has been great – it's distracted me from all that awful Fred situation.'

'But you and Fred are so well suited!' marvelled Luke. 'I can see it now! You'd be just perfect together! Why did you split up? What happened?'

'Well . . .' Jess took a deep breath. 'It was only a couple of weeks ago . . . I dumped him because we'd been trying to organise a dinner dance, and he was totally useless at it and he kept promising to do things and then not doing them, and eventually he said he was "resigning from the committee" – the committee was just me and him, by the way – which really dropped me in it.'

'But . . .' Luke looked puzzled. 'This is Fred, right? I've only met the guy a few times, but it's obvious that, well, organising things isn't his strong point, or am I wrong?'

'Too right!' sighed Jess.

'So, maybe . . . you were expecting him to do stuff that's way out of his range?' asked Luke.

'But I'm totally disorganised, too, and I just had to pull out all the stops and get on with it –'

'No, no,' Luke interrupted. 'Excuse me, but you're totally different from Fred. That's the way it seems to me, anyway. I know you've got the same sense of humour, but you're so confident and he's so shy.'

'Fred, shy?' Jess frowned in puzzlement.

'Lacking in confidence, I'd say, which he covers up with all this comedy stuff,' suggested Luke.

Jess thought about this suggestion for a moment or two. 'You know,' she concluded, 'ever since I dumped him, I've been waiting for him to do something amazing to get back into my good books. You know, take the initiative or something. Or even just apologise properly.'

'You could have a long wait,' said Luke, smiling ruefully. 'I think he's a passive character – he bounces off people; he reacts to situations instead of taking the initiative. So when you dumped him I bet he was filled with terror. He probably didn't dare to make any approaches to you in case you were still mad at him and dumped him all over again, and that would have felt so final. Devastating.'

'I see,' mused Jess. 'But I kind of hate that in him, though – being so passive.'

'But you don't hate Fred, do you? It's just part of his personality. And people do change sometimes. But everybody's got faults.'

'You don't seem to have any,' observed Jess, with a wry grin. 'Fred says you walk on water.'

Luke laughed dismissively. 'I've got the opposite fault to him. I'm a control freak. I'm always rushing into things, trying to force things to happen. Just like with you and me. I was sure we could become an item. I pushed it all along much too fast and it could have been really messy.'

'Not really – I mean, we both knew it wasn't working.'

'But supposing you'd felt differently? I know I'm awful and stuff, but supposing you had got kind of fond of me, you know, it would have been such a let-down for you. And look at the heartache I've caused Sophie. I couldn't stand the uncertainty of her being in Manchester and me down here. That's another thing – I'm so jealous!'

'I think everybody's jealous,' said Jess. 'It's a sign that you're still alive. Like, *does he have a heartbeat? Is he breathing? Is he jealous? Yes, he's breathing and his heart is beating, but he's not jealous. Ah! He must be dead, then!*' They laughed.

'You're so funny!' grinned Luke. 'Sophie would love you!'

'What faults does she have?' asked Jess mischievously.

'Oh.' A foolish smile crept over Luke's face. 'She's totally disorganised and untidy. She leaves everything to the last minute. She's missed more trains than I've had hot dinners. She's always late. She was two hours late for our first date.'

'Two hours!'

'Yes, you see? Completely wrong for me cos I'm the control freak. We're so wrong together, but I can't get her out of my mind. And the film – well, that was all about her, of course. Being haunted by the ex-girlfriend.'

'Well, cheer up! At least she hasn't thrown herself under a train – has she?' Jess enquired.

'No, not as far as I know.'

'Well, text her and tell her you're sorry!'

'I will, I will, but will she forgive me?'

'If she cares enough about you, she will.'

'What a huge mistake I made, dumping her like that . . . Thanks so much, Jess. You've been the best friend a guy could have.'

'And that's what we are,' said Jess firmly. 'Mates, right?'

'Right!' They had a brief hug.

'I was so scared back there for a minute,' admitted Jess as they resumed their walk home. 'I thought you were going to say you loved me!'

'Well, I do love you in a way, of course . . .' began Luke.

'No, no!' grinned Jess. 'Let's just say "*I don't love you*" because sometimes that's what you want to hear.'

'Right, then. I don't love you, Jess. Sorry, it sounds so rude!'

'And I don't love you, either – isn't it great?' Jess squeezed his arm. 'Now we can go home and get on with our lives.'

They strolled on, arm in arm in the moonlight. Jess felt relieved because now at least she knew how she felt, though there was the suspense of not knowing what Fred was going to do. Flora might be able to dump Jack without a backward look, but Jess felt Fred was going to be part of her life for ever. Now Fred was reinventing himself, maybe Jess had to reinvent herself, too. So they could meet next time on new ground, with new rules, with the slate wiped clean, and start over. Except that Jodie was currently Queen of the Castle.

'Jodie's my big problem now,' she murmured. 'Like, can I get Fred back off her – by fair means or foul? I don't want to hurt her feelings. After all, she railroaded him fair and square.'

Luke laughed. 'Don't forget you owe her five pounds,' he said. 'She bet you you would get kissed within a week.'

'Hmmmm.' Jess pondered. 'Shall we just forget that ever happened?'

'OK,' agreed Luke. 'It'll be our little secret.'

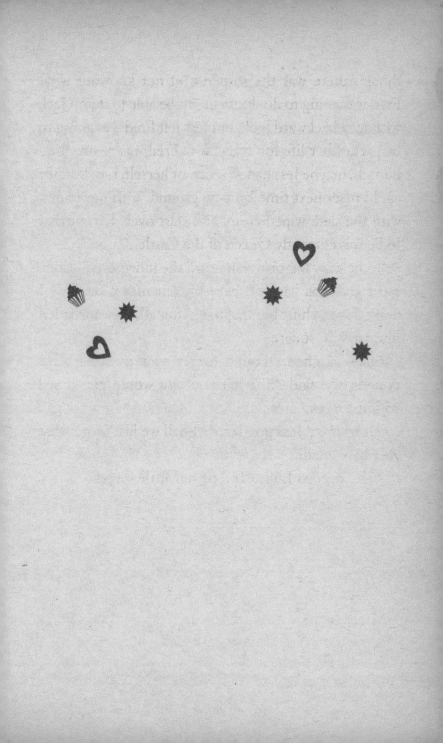

Win a Totally Cool Pink iPad 2

Have you ever nearly just died from embarrassment? Well, you can take that cringe-worthy moment and put it to good use!

Send in a description of your most embarrassing moment (in 50 words or less) to
childrensmarketing@bloomsbury.com
and you will be in with a chance of winning a super-cool pink iPad 2!

You can find out more about this totally awesome competition at **www.JessJordan.co.uk**

Hi, guys!

You're so brilliant reading this and it's really cheered me up, as Fred is being a bit of a toad at the moment — not that he's covered with warts and is shooting poison out of his neck (but give him time). Sometimes I feel that you're my only friend, especially when Flora's at orchestra practice. So please, please, do me a ginormous favour and visit my fabulous, dazzling, low-calorie, high-energy website — **www.JessJordan.co.uk!!!!**

I'm going to be blogging away (I wrote glogging by accident at first and I kind of like it, so I might be glogging too) and I can promise you loads of laughs, polls, quizzes, interactive stuff, downloadable goodies, plus sensational secrets that Fred, Flora, Ben, Mackenzie and Jodie have begged me to never reveal! Don't tell them I sent you — and promise you'll be there!

Love,
Jess!

Get Over Your Ex the Jess Jordan Way

First, treat yourself — chocolate, and plenty of it! But chocolate can also be used a weapon if you follow these easy steps.

 Make a chocolate model of your ex. Bite his head off.

 Go round to his house on laundry day, sneak into the garden and smear his pants with melted chocolate.

* Casually drop a half-melted chocolate bar into his school bag, preferably right on top of his homework.

* Construct a new boyfriend out of chocolate and drive past the bus stop looking glamorous and haughty in a sports car (preferably also made of chocolate).

✻ If you get sick of chocolate, let your ex know what a worm he is by dropping a worm down the back of his neck.

For more top tips from Jess, visit **www.JessJordan.co.uk**

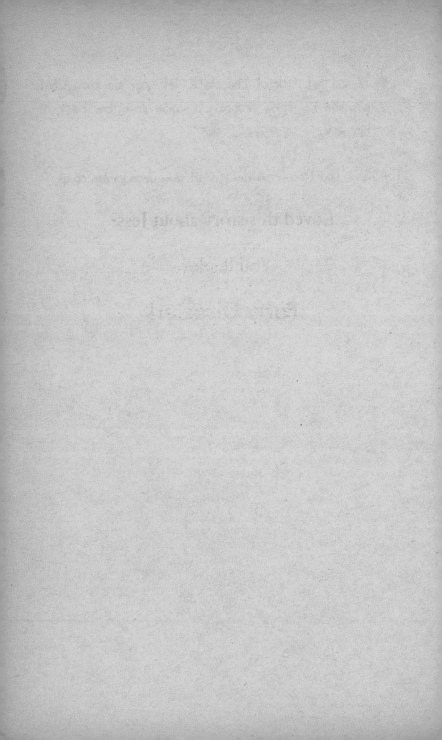

Loved this story about Jess?

You'll adore

Party Disaster!

Chapter 1

Jess sat in her bedroom and wrote a title on a piece of paper: *Reasons to Be Cheerful*. *There have to be some*, she thought desperately. Life had been beastly recently, with Fred behaving – well, behaving like a rat. So what *did* she have to be cheerful about?

Jess stared moodily at the carpet. A tiny beetle ran under her desk. Luckily she didn't mind insects. Just rats, really. Especially the human sort.

1) I'm not a cockroach. A bit of a random reason to be cheerful, but she had to start somewhere. Although it's possible, admitted Jess, that cockroaches have a lifestyle that's one hundred per cent fun, holding all-night raves on the floors of dirty kitchens every night of the year.

2) I'm not obese. During the winter, thick fleeces had kept her bod discreetly veiled, but now spring was here and she was going to have to foist her lard on the unsuspecting public. Her backside was so big, she often had the feeling she was being followed.

3) I'm not seriously ill. Jess paused. She'd better check first. She started by examining her hands. They looked just about OK – at least they hadn't fallen off in the night. Jess became distracted by her fingers. She'd read somewhere that having an index finger shorter than your ring finger meant that you might have some masculine characteristics, such as being good at maths and asserting yourself. Jess sighed. Her index finger was definitely longer than her ring finger, so it was unlikely that she would turn out to be a stylish mathematician with her own TV game show.

4) My mum and dad, though divorced, are friends. Her parents had got divorced when she was too young to remember any of it. Though mad in their own quiet ways, they were so well behaved they'd probably managed not to throw too many plates at each other. If any china had been hurled, it was most likely to have been only egg cups.

5) Granny understands me and is still alive (that is, she was when I last looked). Jess suddenly had a horrid thought and raced downstairs. Granny was sitting in front of the TV, fast asleep with her mouth open. Jess stared anxiously at Granny's chest encased in its cosy hand-knitted cardi emblazoned with a woolly picture of dolphins leaping joyfully in and out of a blue-green sea. Thank goodness! The sea was rising and falling regularly, an infallible sign that Granny was still alive, though Jess did feel a slight pang of seasickness. On the TV somebody was being ill treated by an alien. Granny found sci-fi and horror delightfully soothing. Though tempted to stay and watch the earth being saved from the brink yet again, Jess ran back upstairs. She still hadn't thought of a reason to be really cheerful, something that cancelled out all the annoying stuff.

6) I've never been tortured by aliens. In fact, being tortured by your very own friends was worse, as Jess now realised. She sighed and stared up at her bulletin board. It was adorned with random stuff: photos of terriers skateboarding, some pics of Flora mugging at the camera, trying to pull a horrendous face yet somehow remaining almost illegally beautiful . . . There were no images of Fred. They'd all been stashed away in Jess's drawer. At the thought of Fred, a wave of rage and indignation swept through her.

Jess grabbed a pencil and ripped a piece of blank paper off a pad. She drew a cartoon of Fred, exaggerating his long legs, his short bristly hair, his huge eyes. Next to him she drew a cruel caricature of Jodie, much fatter than she'd ever been in real life, and dolled up in a bride's veil. Above the happy couple, Jess wrote in red felt tip, *You may kick the bride!* Then she pinned it to her bulletin board. *I must get some darts*, she thought. Firing some arrows off at that irritating pair would cheer her up in her worst moments.

Reluctantly she dragged herself away from the wedding pic of Fred and Jodie, and returned to her *Reasons to Be Cheerful*. She really did want to be cheerful again, not kind of smouldering from an inner fire the way she had been for weeks now.

7) *I'm lucky to live in the age of TV.* Imagine all those poor Stone Age people, forced to draw mammoths on cave walls to while away the time. And how did they even play charades in the prehistoric era? You couldn't start with '*is it a book, a film or a movie?*' It would always have been a cave painting, an odd-looking vegetable or a lump of mammoth poo that looked amusingly like somebody's head.

8) *Despite humanity's attempts to ruin the planet, we still have small, furry, cuddly animals. Just not in this actual house*, thought Jess resentfully. Despite a relentless campaign of nagging, she was as far away from having a pet as ever. The nearest thing she had to a small fluffy creature was her fur-trapper's hat which was made of polyester. Maybe it should be known as

a polyester-trapper's hat. She was quite tempted, sometimes, to call it Twinkle and to take it for walks on a lead.

9) I'm not going out with Luke. Although Luke was a really lovely guy, and amazingly talented, for Jess to go out with him would have been wrong, wrong, wrong. She had made the right decision there, at least.

At this point Jess sighed and threw away her pen. She had meant to toss it lightly on to the desk and for it to lie there creating an atmosphere of chic despair. Instead it bounced off the wall and fell down behind the back of the desk. She glared at the cartoon of Fred and Jodie getting married. It gave her a strange, ferocious pleasure. She thought she might do some more drawings of them later. She might invent some horrible children for them, and a vile dog called Frodie who looked a bit like Jodie. And she'd make them live in a nasty house covered with house-warts.

This bitter and twisted mood had to be dispelled somehow! Jess tried to pull herself together. She decided to do the only sensible thing: flip open her laptop, find a tarot website and have her fortune read. She was immediately instructed to *think of a question or an object of concern*. Jess closed her eyes.

How much longer am I going to have to endure this? she begged the invisible Fates. *Will things ever get back to the way they were?*

She'd selected a three-card reading – for the past, present and future. The first card to be revealed represented the past. It was the Five of Swords and symbolised Loss and Regret. 'Too right!' cried Jess aloud. She read on. *Sometimes one has to accept one's errors in judgement and one's rash and belligerent actions.* But had she made an error in judgement?

She looked up *belligerent* on the online dictionary just in case it might mean something not quite as bad as she suspected. *Inclined or eager to fight*, the definition said. *Hostile or aggressive.* She wondered whether she had been hostile or aggressive, or whether she had been perfectly justified when she let rip at Fred during Chaos, the Valentine's dinner dance.

Abandoning the online tarot reading in despair, Jess went downstairs. Granny had woken up from her little nap and was watching avidly as a Special Space Force Agent destroyed some aliens without, miraculously, ruining her hair.

'She's got them on the run now,' Granny commented reassuringly. 'But there's a twist in the tail – they've taken over her partner's body. I've seen this one before.'

'What happens in the end?' asked Jess, flopping down on the hearthrug beside Granny's feet.

'It's one of those coat hanger episodes,' said Granny. 'Cliffhanger, I mean. She finds her mate again and there's this grand reunion, but gradually she realises that he's been taken over by an evil alien force.'

Jess shuddered with recognition. Something very similar had been happening in her own life, ever since Fred had started going out with Jodie.

Get to Know Sue Limb
with her Q & A!

* **Name:** Sue Limb.

* **Star sign:** Virgo.

* **Favourite colour:** Green.

* **Favourite number:** Seven.

* **Favourite thing to do:** Give my dog a bath.

* **Favourite food:** Anything with pesto.

* **Where were you born?** Hitchin, Hertfordshire, England.

* **Where do you live now?** On a remote farm in Gloucestershire.

What were you like at school? A tomboy-ish nerd.

Have you got brothers and sisters? One older brother, who's a jazz musician.

What did you want to be as a child? Secretary-General of the United Nations (I told you I was a nerd).

How did you start writing? At age two, I liked doodling the letter 'S'. When I grew up, I tried teaching, couldn't cope, and writing seemed to be the only thing possible.

What did you do before you were a writer? I was a teacher, screaming in vain for quiet while my classes rioted gently around me.

Where do you write? Anywhere – I particularly like writing on trains. But when I'm at home, in a room with windows opening into a wild wood.

What was your favourite book as a child? *The Railway Children* by E. Nesbit.

* **What's your favourite children's book now?** *Where the Wild Things Are* by Maurice Sendak.

* **What's your favourite adult book?** *Persuasion* by Jane Austen.

* **What tips do you have for budding writers?** Read a lot!

* **What's your favourite TV programme?** *Frasier*.

* **What makes you laugh?** Harry Enfield and Paul Whitehouse as the Surgeons.

* **What's your favourite movie?** *Some Like It Hot*.

* **Who do you imagine playing Jess, Flora and Fred in a movie?** Carey Mulligan would be Jess, Emma Watson would be Flora and Jamie Campbell Bower would be Fred.